OK,
Mr Field

Katharine Kilalea

FABER & FABER

First published in 2018
by Faber & Faber Limited
Bloomsbury House
74–77 Great Russell Street
London, WC1B 3DA

Typeset by Faber & Faber Limited
Printed in the UK by CPI Group (UK) Ltd, Croydon, CR0 4YY

A CIP record for this book
is available from the British Library

ISBN 978-0-571-34087-3

10 9 8 7 6 5 4 3 2 1

For JHC

SUMMER

Chapter 1

Being in the dark
is like being on the inside of
one's own body

I woke to several different noises, something being picked up and put down, a tap being turned on and off. *What time is it?* I said. *It's 4 a.m.*, said Mim. For a moment she was silhouetted in the bathroom door before the light went off and she was reabsorbed into the dark. Outside, the sky was so black that when I looked at it I was looking at nothing but my memory of the sky. Were it not for the moon shining through the narrow band of windows, I couldn't say whether my eyes were closed or open.

The church bells rang four times down in the bay. I stuck my foot out from under the covers and tried to sleep, but my head was full of night-time voices overtaking and interrupting one another so it sounded like there were many voices talking at once though really it was just the same voice repeating the same few meaningless questions – *What month is it? Clytemnestra? Who was Tchaikovsky's son?* – which, in any case, were impossible to answer since each one seemed to dissolve the moment it caught my attention.

Lying there, the quiet was disturbed by the sound of Mim's footsteps toing and froing on the ceiling above me. *You're too sensitive*, said a voice inside my head. *It's just Mim, walking.* So I rolled over and closed my eyes but on my side the sound of her footsteps dropped down in a straight line from the ceiling into my ear where, having penetrated my head, they made a right turn and took root in my sternum before infecting my heart, which started beating louder and faster than before. *Relax*, I told my heart, *there's nothing to worry about.* But of course a heart doesn't understand human language and the only way to still it is by force, which I did, wrapping my arms tightly over my chest, though each time I drifted off my grip relaxed and the thudding, unsuppressed, would startle me awake again. *Don't just lie there*, the voice said. *Why don't you do something? Why don't you find her and ask her what the matter is?*

Because sometimes, I thought, *it's better not to know.*

I must eventually have grown immune to Mim's pacing because the church bells rang five times in the bay but by six o'clock they'd been incorporated into a dream in which I, in a concert hall, was about to premiere a concerto by a celebrated composer. The orchestra had already started but I was waiting for the conductor to bring me in, which presently he did, gesturing at me with his baton. I put my hands on the piano but when I looked up at the score all I saw was a jar of peanut butter. The next page had no musical notation either, just more pictures of peanut butter. *Don't just sit there*, the conductor hissed. *Do something!* So I took my hands off the piano again and said, *Peanut butter.* And then, because what else was there to do, I said, *Peanut butter* again. *Peanut butter, peanut butter, peanut butter . . .* I said. And the orchestra, lowering their instruments, started chanting, *Peanut butter, peanut butter, peanut butter . . .* too.

The mood of foreboding left over from the dream dissolved the moment it was exposed to the pitiless light flooding through the bedroom windows. I pushed past the mouldy blue plastic curtain separating the bathroom from the bedroom, went to the toilet, and felt empty. It was only eight o'clock – the church bells rang eight times in the bay – but I felt disoriented, as though I'd slept right through the day into the following night. The remains of Mim's bathwater were lukewarm, neither hot enough to be comforting nor cold enough to jolt me out of the fog of oversleeping.

I pulled the plug and the pipes behind the house shuddered and moaned as they drained away the grey water. Like everything in the house, the blue mosaic bath was a replica of the one in the Villa Savoye. The house was one of three Villa Savoye doppelgängers: there was the 'shadow' version in Canberra, which was an exact copy but painted black; the 'mini' Villa Savoye in Boston, in which every aspect of the original had been shrunk by 10 per cent to fit the client's budget, and my house, the House for the Study of Water, which replicated Le Corbusier's in all aspects apart from its location since the original Villa Savoye overlooks the rural French landscape, while the one in Cape Town overlooked the sea.

Everything I knew about Le Corbusier came from a South African academic who, like a number of so-called architourists, had turned up at the house one day as though it were a museum rather than a private residence. She wore a kaftan and jangly bracelets and was writing a book, she told me, on Le Corbusier and the 'third world'. The architect who'd designed the House for the Study of Water, Jan Kallenbach, had met Le Corbusier during a tour which he and several other architecture students had made of European architecture. They'd turned up at Le Corbusier's apartment one day, she said, and the old architect had invited them in and said, *OK* – she mimicked his French accent – *so now I will teach you the système*. The *système* entailed a number of rules which Le Corbusier applied to all buildings, regardless of their size or use, like that all buildings should have movable walls, a roof terrace, horizontal windows and be raised off the ground on stilts. The architecture students – later known as the Johannesburg Group – published articles on Le Corbusier's *système* in the local journal, *South Africa Architectural Record*, and applied it to the design of a number of new houses, built mostly for German Jewish immigrants who'd developed a taste for modernism before the war. With their glass walls and external staircases, these houses typified what became known as the Johannesburg Style. *The point about the houses*, she said – this must have been important because she repeated it several times – *is that they were 'à la Corbu' but not just meaningless copies. They took his system and synthesised it in a new way*. Whereas Kallenbach, apparently, had been so seduced by the Master, as he'd called him, that he believed the practice of architecture post-Le Corbusier could offer nothing more than to replicate his buildings verbatim. We were standing at the strip of windows in the living room, looking at the sea. *That's why he was ostracised from the inner circle*, she said. Then she turned away from the window. *I feel queasy*, she said. *The way these windows cut off the ground makes me feel seasick.* And for a moment she did look pale, but then, laughing, went on. *Maybe* that's *the reason Kallenbach's wife left him. Because living here was like living on a raft.* It's true, the windows did give one an odd perspective of the world. I'd often thought it perverse that a house overlooking the sea should have windows so narrow that they hid all but a sliver of it. It was a restrictive view, almost punitively so, so frustratingly partial that it seemed a kind of tease. Though the sense of something withheld – the sea was there, of course, you just couldn't see it – was not entirely unpleasant.

My first encounter with the House for the Study of Water had been on an overheated train several months earlier. I was returning from a recital in which I'd played a prelude by Chopin. The performance had gone badly, a failure I blamed partly on the piano (which I'd not had a chance to familiarise myself with beforehand) and partly on playing directly after the improbably named Belinda Carrots – *the standout pianist of our generation*, newspapers called her – to whom I was certain that some terrible thing had happened because every time I heard her I just felt so sad.

The venue was makeshift, an old London courtroom with a piano in it. I had played Chopin's Raindrop Prelude, a piece which most pianists find appallingly sentimental but I, for whatever reason one falls in love with a piece of music, had loved since the moment I first heard it. I'd sat down and, as was my habit, closed my eyes. *What's he doing?* someone (deaf or senile, perhaps) had whispered. And what was I doing? I was thinking about Chopin. I was imagining his situation. I was trying to let his feelings, by force of will, enter my body. By the time I started – the melody began in a minor key – I had relocated myself from the brightly lit courtroom where I was sitting to the damp Majorcan monastery where Chopin, pale, dark-haired, tubercular, had installed the piano he'd shipped over from Prague. It was raining. Chopin was waiting for his lover, George Sand, to return with a doctor. The gentle and elegiac melody was, to a certain extent, an expression of the weather, or his feelings about it. When the rain swelled the melody got darker; when the rain relented, Chopin – thinking the storm was withdrawing – made it sweeter and more harmonious. A single A flat note, repeated predominantly by the left hand throughout the piece, represented the sound of the rain from inside the house. While I was playing I was imagining Chopin, himself imagining Sand, or her carriage capsized somewhere along the mountain path, and my chest sank down over the piano in sympathy with his situation. What made the story so awful wasn't the rain or the cold or the illness, what was worse was the waiting. The waiting made my heart accelerate and caused my fingers, since the heart is the body's metronome, to follow suit, rushing faster and harder over the keys until they hammered the instrument with such urgency that they seemed not so much to be playing it as trying to penetrate it, to break through to its interior, to burrow into its deepest, most inscrutable recesses, the parts of it where I'd not been before. My right foot rested on the pedal. All around me in the airless courtroom were muddy undifferentiated sounds hanging in the air. The prelude – or that of it which emerged through the wash of notes – mingled with sounds of phlegmy coughs and people shuffling around. *Show-off!* someone whispered. And I must have been really pounding the piano because as the storm reached its climax it literally came to pieces, the beading falling off and landing on the floor with a clatter.

Afterwards, paging through the newspaper at the far end of an empty train carriage, I saw a photograph of the house: a brilliant white box raised off the ground on stilts, with curvy sculptural shapes on its roof. The article wasn't about the house, it was about the death of the minor South African architect who'd built it. It was more a light-relief piece than an obituary, syndicated from a local paper on the strength, I expect, of its macabre headline, *All That Was Left Was His Red Swimming Cap*. There was an interview with a fisherman who'd witnessed the attack. *I saw him wading into the water*, he said. *When I came back a few minutes later the water was churning. At first I thought it was a shark eating a seal but there was a lot of blood. By the time I called the ambulance, all that was left was his red swimming cap.*

As the train was about to leave, a well-dressed couple slipped in through the closing doors. It was impossible not to hear, even through the noise of the train moving, that they were talking about me. *I can't explain it*, the man said. *I can't explain it . . .* He spoke slowly, as if searching for exactly the right words. *The way he played was just so . . . so . . .*

Unmusical? the woman said.

Yes, he said, *horrible. Mechanical, even. Yet somehow also heartbreaking. It wasn't the playing itself which was sad – I mean there was nothing sad about his phrasing or his interpretation – what was so moving was, how do I say it, well, it's as if what was so moving was his absence of feeling. The way he turned the piece into a splintered, wooden rendition of itself. As if he hated the piece,* he said, *and didn't want to be playing it. And do you know,* the man went on, *that when we passed him in the foyer after the performance a strange thing happened. I heard him talking and the way he talks is exactly the same – dull, but almost deliberately so, as if he didn't really mean what he was saying. Or doesn't understand the pauses or emphases a person uses to convey a feeling.*

The couple got off and a man with a violin case got on. His eyes were tired and he was so roughly dressed that you couldn't say whether he was a busker or a music student. I was sitting with my jacket on my lap and my scarf on my jacket and my old leather music satchel on top of that, on which, lying open, was the newspaper, whose pages I had all the while kept turning to avoid being recognised. *So they didn't like me,* I thought. *Well, I didn't like them either.* But the words in the newspaper swelled and shrunk as though the page beneath me were breathing.

From time to time, as the train passed through the dark underground tunnels, a ceiling vent opened, letting warm gusts into the carriage, which, if I closed my eyes and let myself believe it, momentarily transported me to somewhere else, somewhere summery. The picture of the house, with its clean lines and pure geometry, was imprinted on the backs of my eyelids. Something about it – the delicacy of the columns holding it up perhaps or the curved shapes on its roof which, contrasted with the restrained mass of the box beneath it, gave the image an almost lyrical flourish – produced a feeling in me: it was similar to love only it wasn't love because I wasn't entertaining loving feelings for anyone nor was there anyone in my mind whom I wished to be loved by. It was just a feeling which *felt like* love, though it was stronger than love and more potent because there was nobody towards whom I could direct and thereby discharge it. I started to doze off. Perhaps it was the heat in the carriage that made me sleepy. Perhaps it was all that weight on my lap, or the rhythm of the tracks, because people around me were falling asleep too in their different ways, some dropping their heads and letting their eyes close, others just staring ahead at the stations passing without really noticing them.

The sleep I fell into was heavy, like the temporary shutting-down a computer does when it goes into sleep mode to conserve energy. I missed my stop and several after it and woke to a loud bang and everyone talking and shouting at once. I remember someone picked me up and carried me like a dog up a long escalator. I remember a tide of commuters climbing over turnstiles. The next thing I remember is coming to in a hospital ward with my left arm bandaged to the elbow. *You were in an accident*, said the doctor at my bedside. *But don't look so worried, I'm not going to cut off your hand.* He laughed and the nurse beside him laughed too. Even the patient in the adjacent bed, whose head had until now been dropped forward as though he were asleep, started laughing though he may have been coughing, I couldn't be sure because he covered his face with his hands. The bones of my left wrist had splintered, I was told, and were now held together by a metal pin, the presence of which, since I couldn't see it (though the bandage confirmed its existence), infected everything with a Gothic atmosphere, making the bloody gauze which the nurse lifted from my skin, hissing through her teeth, look like a stringy spiderweb spanning the lips of the cut, and the fluid seeping from a stitch look like oil oozing from a grotesque sausage.

The accident must have been in the news because I heard two nurses smoking in the covered walkway outside my window talking about it. *It must have been suicide*, one was saying, *because the driver died with his hand on the accelerator.*

What's inconceivable to me, said the other, *is the wad of cash in his pocket. He'd withdrawn it to buy his daughter a car. Who kills himself when he's planning to buy his daughter a car?*

The first nurse looked at her cigarette as if it had suddenly become distasteful. *Yes*, she said, *but who drives into a brick wall and doesn't cover his face with his hands?*

Anyway, said the other, *life is short and then you die. Sometimes I wish I were just a train driver, so I could drive around all day listening to music . . .*

Chapter 2

The front door

A gloomy twilight filtered in through the blue plastic curtain. When the curtain was closed the bathroom had a romantic charm, but in the blinding light when it was drawn to one side the rusty taps and ominous floor puddles made it resemble a neglected urinal. Every day the face I encountered in the mirror looked more and more decayed. The mouth sagged, the beard poked out in different directions, the forehead seemed to fall away from the bones beneath it. The eyes I met were mapped with thin red veins branching, like a crack left unattended, from the whites of the eyeballs into the skin around them. They watched me with a steady gaze, a gaze that seemed to carry the weight of some understanding.

I looked at myself so intently and for so long that, as happens when one is tired or has been looking at oneself for some time, I saw myself from a distance as if I were someone else. *How sad he looks*, that inner voice commented. *How sad he looks, standing there. About whom? About what?* But the answer was stalled by the appearance of a strange cloud passing by the window. It was bright red, like the sunset clouds in fairy tales, and I stared at the window in case it appeared again, which it did, only this time it was preceded by a helicopter, and followed by several more helicopters. In fact, the sky was full of helicopters. I watched them appear and disappear, carrying seawater to a fire somewhere on the other side of the mountain. There had been no rain for months and the grass in the garden was dying even as I looked at it. Joggers jogged along the coastal path with their shirts tucked into their waistbands. Behind them was the sea.

It was some time ago now but I thought of the day I'd arrived in Cape Town. I was alone – Mim would follow some weeks later – and the sun was shining brightly through the blueness of a summer's afternoon as I made my way along the overpass past the harbour, with its cranes and shipping cargo, to the house where Jan Kallenbach's widow now lived. How different it was from the white house on the mountain! I parked on the small tree-lined avenue and sat for a while looking through the fence at her large house, whose Cape Dutch gables rose in memory of another time. The combined effect of jet lag and caffeine and the dappled light coming through the trees made me acutely sensitive so that when I pressed the brass filigreed doorbell, the harsh buzz it discharged into the house – so at odds with the bell's genteel appearance – made me jump back as though I'd been electrocuted. I rang twice and still was left waiting. When the door finally opened it didn't open completely but stood slightly ajar for a moment before a woman appeared, her face peering through the gap like a puppet leaning out from the wings of a puppet show. *Oh, it's you*, Kallenbach's widow said, observing me through the crack. When she drew the door back she was older than I'd expected, older yet more elegant. There was no smile or extended hand, just this widening of the door, which made the greeting not unfriendly but oddly familiar, less a stranger's welcome than the way you'd address a family member who'd stepped out for a moment.

Do come in, Hannah Kallenbach said, with an emphasis on *do*. I followed her across the entrance hall and down a corridor towards the back of the house. She faced directly ahead, not turning to check whether I was still behind her, her trim legs making neat, purposeful steps. The black jacket she wore was unusually severe for a woman her age: it ballooned from her body like the bomber jackets worn by doormen at certain expensive restaurants.

The small room at the back of the house had high ceilings and was warmly furnished in no particular style. Hannah Kallenbach gestured to a string-bound chair in the corner and sat down across from me in a chair that was similar to mine, only more weathered. Two long-legged spiders dangled from the ceiling above her. She observed me through narrowing eyes, the muscles around her eyeballs contracting very slightly as though focusing on something very small or squinting against the sun. I turned away to survey the room. Under the window was a heavy mahogany desk with brass half-moon handles on the drawers down either side. Beside me was a wall-to-wall bookshelf full of books – big books, the kind of grand European novels which concern themselves with the human condition. Otherwise the space was decorated with only a few mismatched ceramic pots and a vase of hyacinths that infused the room with a sickly, sensual smell, the heat of the day having loosened their petals and released their scents and moistures into the air. The atmosphere was close. Perhaps it was the walls, which had been painted a shade of cream so rich it was almost yellow, a colour which caught the sunlight and softened it, giving everything a luminosity and making the room feel intimate, as though I'd come on personal rather than professional business.

We were sitting now, on either side of the room, she with her profile sharply defined by the light coming in through the open window, before which, facing one another, we sat. On her desk were papers and a pile of CDs, Brahms recordings. *Why does she like Brahms so much?* I wondered. Because I didn't like Brahms. When I listened to Brahms I always felt I was wasting my time. In the silence which opened up I became aware of an uncanny feeling, as if the room I'd entered was not a stranger's room but my own, only a room I'd known or lived in so long ago that I'd lost all memory of it. I wanted to say something or make some noise to express this feeling but what to say was unclear, and in any case the feeling was almost immediately replaced by a sort of heaviness, a sadness, even, but a small one, not one whose source I could immediately identify. A wish for something, perhaps. Not something outlandish, something tangible, something I could have had if only I were quicker or bolder or different somehow. *Hmm*, I said. It was a nice sound. Like an engine starting some-where deep inside. *Hmm.*

Are you an architect? Hannah Kallenbach asked. *No,* I said, *I know nothing about architecture.*

But you do know, she said, *that the house was designed as a holiday house? That it was never meant to be lived in.*

As Hannah Kallenbach reached into the drawer of her heavy mahogany desk – *I made a list of people who might be useful to you,* she said, *but where's the piece of paper where I wrote it down?* – my mind returned to the evening I told Mim how I'd spent my compensa-tion payout. We were eating artichokes. *The Villa what?* she'd said, tapping salt into her hand. *Savoye?* she asked. *Savoye? S-A-V-O-Y-E?*, as though it was the word rath-er than its meaning that mattered. *I know Savoie,* she said, *we went skiing there as a child. The food was ter-rible.* Then she mumbled what sounded like *savoir faire* and ruffled her hair and laughed a laugh that betrayed the hateful things she thought about me. *What do you like about this house so much anyway?* she said, and I said, *I don't know.* Why did I like the house? Who knows. A man feels what he feels and he can't feel anything else. *I just like it, or admire it, or something,* I said. But those were bland words, too fearful, too subtle to describe my feelings. *Something about it is just wonderful,* I said. But what makes something wonderful? *Nothing in life is really wonderful,* said Mim, as though my wishing it so were the source of all her disappointment.

Hannah Kallenbach handed me the keys to the house. As I stood to leave, my eyes were drawn, not for the first time, to the painting on the wall behind me, which I had taken at first for a child's drawing but now realised was a print by Chagall or someone after Chagall, whose childlike affect came from the crude style in which its three main figures – a woman, a dog and a house – had been drawn. They were representations of types: the sad woman, the friendly dog and the kind of rudimentary house – a box with a front door and smoking chimney – which nursery-school children draw. The woman's hand was pressed to her chest and she was looking to one side. Her eyes were slits, as if she'd half-closed them or was looking into the distance. The dog wore a mild expression and its innocent-looking face was so round – a bubble of a face – that it seemed to have no snout. Behind them was a swirl of faint blue paint, as if they were immersed in water. None of them seemed aware of each other's presence, they were just floating there, suspended in the pale-blue paint, dreaming or reminiscing perhaps, with their edges partly obscured by the blue so it was hard to say which was the foreground or the background, the figures or the blue paint, and which had been painted first. The painting had a sketchy quality, as though the artist had been in too much of a rush to get it finished. The boundaries of the figures trailed off in places. The woman's arm, which was folded over her body, had lost its outline at the forearm and seemed to melt into her chest, while the dog's legs, fading below the knees, merged with the roof of the house beneath. There were gaps where the four lines representing the walls of the house didn't meet up, in the corners, which I couldn't help mentally 'plugging up' to stop the house's contents from seeping out. I stood there for a moment, looking at the woman, herself gazing, as if lost in a daydream, at something I couldn't see beyond the picture frame, while the dog in turn gazed at her with his large and compassionate eyes, his expression, like hers, suggesting that he was not looking at her but looking at nothing, just resting his eyes on her while lost in thought. And I must have taken off my jacket because then I'd put it on again, awkwardly, ruching the sleeves of my shirt in my hurry to bundle myself back into the packaging I'd arrived in.

The leather seat was moist when I returned to the car.

Following Hannah Kallenbach's directions, I drove out along the highway for an hour or so before turning onto a smaller mountain road that wound its way towards the house in tight curves. I caught myself thinking, from time to time, about the woman in the painting. Her predicament was compelling. It seemed to me, from the way her eyes gazed longingly towards whatever was beyond the picture frame, that she was missing home. What was she looking at? The only way to find out, I thought, would be to take her off the canvas and ask her. I had the idea that Russia was home because she wore the same style of headscarf as the Russian woman – educated under Stalinism – who'd taught me piano as a boy, a pale woman with pockmarked skin who'd practised so hard that she could play Czerny by heart while reading a novel. Beside the road were fleshy succulents and trumpet-shaped red flowers I couldn't name. A few buck grazed here and there on the mountainside. The road twisted past a cluster of rudimentary red-brick school buildings and a low-rise concrete military hospital tucked inside a forest of blue gum trees, tilted to the wind. Then it narrowed and rose sharply upwards, angled so steeply towards the top of the mountain that the hire car's little engine struggled noisily and I turned off the air-con to help it. I opened the window. The coast was nearing; I couldn't see it but I knew it was there because there was a sea smell in the air. The car edged so slowly up the incline that a queue of motorists was piling up behind me, and just as I feared it was about to give up completely the road levelled out, giving way to sea stretching in every direction. As the view opened up I felt something inside me open up too, as though while my eyes stretched out towards the horizon an equal gaze was extending back in, reversing from my eyeballs to the depths of my skull. How wonderful it was to have nothing to look at! *How long have I longed for this*, I thought. *How many times, in London, where everywhere you look there is a building or a bus in your line of vision, have I longed to stretch my eyes into the distance? How many times have I thought that in a city one has no sense of perspective, that with no sense of perspective, one has no space to think?*

WELCOME TO FALSE BAY, a sign said. As the car passed from one side of the mountain to the other, the landscape went from tropical to arid, from fleshy to brittle, as though I'd entered another country with different plants and different animals and different flowers. Signs lined the road: SLOW DOWN PLEASE! CAUTION PORCUPINES! DANGER FALLING ROCKS! BEWARE POTHOLES! Something rousing was playing on the radio, something by Mahler, and as the car bumped along the tarmac, which hadn't been resurfaced for some time, I bounced around in my seat in a kind of involuntary dance. As the narrow road dropped to sea level, hugging the peninsula, the town came in and out of view across the bay. I passed roads whose names – Capri Road, Warwick Street, Edinburgh Drive – recalled the wealthy European settlers who'd holidayed almost a century earlier in what was then known as the Cape Riviera. Most of their sprawling villas huddled against the mountain had been converted into youth hostels or care homes. I passed a boarded-up Edwardian railway station and a strip of beach, a row of colourful but tired Victorian bathing huts whose paintwork looked untouched since they were built. Then, on a distant slope, the house appeared. The grand white box, as in the photograph in the newspaper, rising from the rocks on its thin white stilts as if signifying, albeit tenuously, the victory of architecture over nature. From afar, the house's stark geometry stood in such sharp contrast to the style of the neighbouring houses – mostly colonial villas adapted for the local climate, Edwardian terraces with louvred windows or Mediterranean villas with thatch roofs – that its presence seemed a form of critique. In the setting sun its walls were luminous, as if lit from within by a fluorescent bulb.

Unlike the Villa Savoye, which is approached by car, the House for the Study of Water was on too steep an incline to drive up and had to be reached by a staircase called Jacob's Ladder. *At my age*, Hannah Kallenbach had said, *that many stairs make life not worth living. I'd have installed some kind of electric funicular system.* At the top of the stairs I found a garden in disrepair and a filled-in fish pond. My first impression of the house itself, in its actuality, was that it was much smaller than it had looked in photographs. The exterior plaster was weary and sad, with cracks spreading across its surface. I wandered around looking for the entrance, which eventually I found around the back of the house.

I had to push past the layer of overgrown ivy which covered the front door as if to deter unwanted guests. Flanking the entrance hall were a ramp and a spiral staircase, while a corridor directly ahead of me led past a small washbasin, the kind for hands, to a door set slightly off-centre at its far end. Assuming a horizontal organisation, I made my way down the corridor towards the door, which opened onto what looked like a disused laundry. Then I backtracked and ascended the ramp that led to the first floor. The white walls flanking the ramp were crumbly and stained, but decorated with patches of light and shadow cast by the striations of the reinforced-glass windows and the vertical lines of radiator bars overhead. A long blue corridor led off the first-floor landing towards the bedrooms, kitchen and living areas. Here and there were traces of the house's previous occupants: something black on the bedroom floor (a rat, I thought, but in fact it was a leather glove), a jar of instant coffee so old its contents had congealed into a single mass. A glass wall separated the living room from a first-floor courtyard whose presence, since it was enclosed by the same ribbon-shaped windows as the rest of the house, I'd not detected from outside. There was some furniture in the living room – a chaise longue, an armchair – but not enough to make the oversized space appear any less institutional.

The ramp continued its journey from the courtyard, rising along the exterior of the house before turning back on itself towards the roof. The final section, hemmed in on one side by head-height walls, terminated at an S-shaped wall enclosing the sea-facing side of the solarium. In the middle of the wall was a hole whose placement, at the end of the ramp, suggested that it was, if not the reward, then at least some compensation for the arduous climb. Unlike the windows in the lower levels of the house, this uppermost aperture was tall, framing a view of the sea so picturesque it might've been a product of my imagination. A concrete slab projected from beneath the window: a table, I supposed, but one with a certain contradictoriness in it, since measured against other tables it seemed too small, and anyway, if it was a table then where were the chairs? In the absence of chairs it seemed logical to rest on top of the slab as if on a high bench, a position which was presumably at odds with the architect's intentions since it oriented me with my back to the view (which, in any case, was difficult to appreciate since the afternoon sun shone so brightly off the water that it hurt my eyes to look). *I don't know, I don't know*, I said. Because on the one hand, it seemed a pity to have reached what was clearly the high point of the house only to turn away from it. But wasn't it also just a relief to let my legs go for a minute? After all, I'd been climbing non-stop since arriving at the house, so, really, sitting down was not a bad outcome at all.

Chapter 3

The word 'hole'

The sun was shining brightly off the whiteness of the page before me when I opened the newspaper. It was hot. Watery noises rose from the tide pool where children were swimming. The silence was otherwise disturbed only by occasional shouts from their strident games mistress who, since the narrow windows encircling the courtyard hid the upper and lower reaches of the world from view, I could hear but not see.

My gaze rested on the newspaper in front of me, whose pages I turned without thinking. The headlines (the news was always about the heatwave or the cricket) were immaterial to me. I had only a vague sense of what was going on. The news interested me only insofar as it provided something to look at and I let my eyes engage momentarily with this or that piece of information, not so much reading as giving them something to do to pass the time. Then I placed the paper face down on the table, stood up and sat down again.

I'd never liked crosswords or any kind of word games. It was a musician's sensibility, perhaps, which made me pay more attention to the sounds of words than to their meanings. I couldn't even read a novel since before long I'd always find myself in the middle of a sentence or a paragraph with no idea of where I was or what had come before. Tracing a plot or following a cast of characters required a mental gymnastics my mind seemed incapable of. Yet that morning, beneath the obituaries and the classifieds, the crossword drew me in. *Who invented the telephone? What nationality was the first dog in space?* My hand picked up the pen as if of its own accord. It felt pleasurable to be filling in the empty grid. It felt like *doing something*, a meaningful activity. Like work, even, to be exerting effort and producing results. The answers came easy at first. But one question led to another and sometimes, beneath the crossword questions, I detected other questions, small, half-formulated questions, questions that were almost too vague to warrant my attention. *Why do you just sit there? Why don't you go out? Why don't you go for a walk or sit in the garden?* But it was too hot to be out-side and the grass was full of ants from the figs that had fallen from the tree. And what is the point of walking when there is nowhere you have to be? So I returned to the crossword, which wasn't as inviting as before. The boxes looked somehow sinister and without purpose. Like moulds, or the husks left over from something that had been there once and been taken away. *Like holes*, I thought. Empty holes. I said the word *hole*. *Hole*. Said out loud, it led in two directions: *Hole*. *Whole*. There was something about it that my ear liked.

A worm shrinked and shrugged its way along the raised flowerbed beside me. Half a dozen cigarette butts were balanced on a leaf of a nearby hydrangea but I didn't look at them or think about them or ask myself why Mim had resumed smoking, which she'd given up for some time. I saw sailboats tacking across the bay, their sails facing away from where they were headed. The way the windows cut off the lower half of the view made the boats seem nearer than they really were, as though they were right there, sailing through the gar-den. But at the same time the illusion of proximity made them seem very far away, since unlike whoever was on board raising the sails or taking the helm or doing what-ever people do on boats, I was just sitting there. *You ought to be doing something*, said the voice in my head. *You should be playing the piano or sailing a boat or something*. But these were idle fantasies. *What would a man like me be doing on a boat anyway*, I thought. *Not raising the mast or taking the helm. I'd just be waiting for the boat to dock so I could sit down somewhere and have a drink.*

My thoughts were interrupted when all the children in the tide pool started screaming at once. I looked down, thinking a fight had broken out, but it hadn't, they were just screaming in pleasure as they threw themselves into the icy water. A particular boy caught my attention. He was standing on the wall in a pair of swimming shorts that made his legs look very small. *What are you waiting for?* the games mistress was saying. *You've got to wet your whole body then you'll be fine*. I stood at the window, feeling the sun pouring into my own body, filling my head and my chest and my shoulders until the temperature inside me was the same as the temperature outside. The tide pool was a confused soup of bodies, one child's limbs hard to disentangle from another's. It felt, standing there, as though the heat was bringing me out of myself the way that, in summer, warm weather brings people out of their houses to spend time in the garden or out of their clothes to spend time in a swimming costume. Then a movement in my peripheral vision caught my eye. Behind the glass wall Mim was making her way down the ramp. She was facing me and I could see her lips moving but the glass between us cut off her voice. As in a silent film, the absence of sound drew attention to her body. There was something strange about the way she moved, chest first and legs trailing behind as if she wasn't in control of herself but being sucked forward into a vacuum that had opened up in the air in front of her.

I followed Mim down the ramp and across the entrance hall towards the laundry at the back of the house, which she'd repurposed as a study. At the end of the corridor she looked at me, as if about to reiterate whatever she'd been saying, then turned away and closed the door behind her. I stared at the laundry door, the angled floor tiles pointed toward it like arrows. It pained me, this door; there were hopes there, fragile hopes I didn't entirely understand. The laundry pulled me toward itself even as it closed its door against me. I'd been standing there for some time when I heard somebody knocking on the front door, but instead of turning around to open it, my feet, as if powered by some external force, carried me down the corridor. Strange thoughts floated into my mind, the vague and fleeting kinds of associations that arrive when one's eyes lose focus, as when looking out the window of a train. Not for the first time, the thought of Hannah Kallenbach occurred to me. Perhaps the house had ingested some aspect of her presence because several times, in the middle of some everyday activity, I'd had the feeling that she was standing there, watching me, so that not infrequently, as I wandered around doing whatever I was doing, I would find myself thinking *What would Hannah Kallenbach think of this?* or *What would Hannah Kallenbach say about that?*

I reached the laundry and stopped, my attention fixed on the door handle, which was tarnished and slightly cocked. *Well*, said Hannah Kallenbach, *what are you waiting for? If you want to see her, why then do you not knock?* But my fingers gripped my trousers so tightly that they felt almost paralysed. From behind the door came computer noises and the sound of Mim's desk chair rolling across the floor. *She knows I'm here*, I thought, *so if she wants to see me, she'll come and get me.* Once, the militant sounds of her typing halted for a moment and my heart stiffened, but the door didn't open.

From behind me came another knock, louder now, but when I turned back to open the door there was nobody there, or rather I didn't see the visitor immediately because he was standing to one side looking away from me towards something out of sight. The ivy that had been tethered to the door lay in a heap on the ground, leaving its small brown footprints on the wall. *Hello?* I said. And then *Hello?* again. The man looked around in surprise, as though I and not he was the unexpected guest. He wore a waistcoat and the baggy orange trousers a handyman wears, with pockets down both sides. His hair was curly, the kind which people like to call a *mop* of curls, though what it most resembled was an old tennis ball. His fleshy and rather froggy features made him look friendly, or if not friendly then at least unthreatening. Before he could speak, coming round the gravel path, a woman appeared in a bright patchwork dress and rubber shoes, so that together, in their colourful outfits, one might mistake them for members of a circus troupe.

The name CURTIS TOUW rose from the business card he produced from one of his many trouser pockets. *We've come about the plot*, he said. They were coming to see everyone in the neighbourhood. The Touws accompanied me up the ramp to the courtyard, where we sat down at the table, each facing slightly different directions because the slab was too low to fit our legs under without angling the chairs to one side. Touw leant in and drew breath as if to start speaking, then pulled away, struggling to find words for what he had to tell me. He seemed to want to convey, through his difficultly in talking, the importance of whatever it was he'd come to say. *How shall I begin?* he seemed to be thinking. *No, not like this.* Several times he repeated this davening motion while, beside him, the woman extracted a number of black sketchbooks from his shoulder bag and laid them with exquisite care in rows on the table, as if preparing a card trick. *The sea is very rhythmic today*, she said, to which he replied, *It's not that rhythmic, actually.*

Resting his hand for a moment on one of the notebooks, Touw pushed it towards me. The first page was blank. On the second page, in an almost illegible calligraphic script, was written *Manifesto for a House in the Sky*. On the third page was a mountain painted in a grandiose style. It had a crystalline shape and no base, so that it seemed to hover, floating, in the clouds. Its outline had been sketched in pencil and filled in with watercolour inks – taupe, yellow and grey – which seeped out in places. *Did you know what you wanted to be when you were a child?* Touw said, and I said, *No.* Which wasn't true because when I was a boy I'd wanted to play the oboe but my mother, who'd found the sound of air being squeezed through a tiny hole painful to listen to, had bought me a piano instead. *Nobody wants to hear about your personal trials and griefs*, she'd said. *Your trials and griefs are boring.*

When I was a child, Touw said, *I wanted to make people happier. So my teachers said I should be a psychologist. But then I found out that all a psychologist does is sit in a room all day, talking. And what's the use of talking? There's no use in talking. I wanted to make things happen.* His wife opened her own notebook and transcribed this. While he was speaking, Touw's eyes had wandered to the fenced-off area of land behind the house. The plot had been empty since I arrived, a razed patch of earth with a corrugated-metal hut to one side whose door sometimes rattled in the wind. A sign was affixed to its gate reading:

CAUTION
INCOMPLETE SITE
RISK OF ACCIDENT

Behind the plot was the mountain. It had the same features as the watercolour mountain in the notebook – the same granite peak with its few sideways-leaning trees, the lonely hiking trail cutting through the ferns – but it was less dreamy-looking so I hadn't recognised it right away. The real mountain was heavy and angular whereas the watercolour version was light and ephemeral, with a more expressive profile. The watercolour mountain looked taller and sharper than the real one, perhaps because Touw had painted the vegetation line lower than it really was to emphasise the rock face and make it seem more brooding. Water from the painted waterfall fell more spectacularly than in actuality, cascading down the rocks, releasing clouds of vapour into the air as it hit the pool. Above, on the bare grey rocks of the highest peak, was painted a cap of shiny snow whose exaggerated whiteness, as in a religious painting, made the top of the mountain stand out against the sky. *But where are the houses?* I asked, because the sprawling colonial villas dotting the mountainside had either been demolished or wished away and replaced by what appeared to be a dozen or so Alpine cowsheds. *The houses were too big and too far apart*, said Touw. The next page showed a close-up of several cowsheds arranged side by side in a circle. *Most people say smallness is bad*, he said, *but I say smallness is good. Most people want big houses but I think a house is a place for living in so it should bring people closer together. How can we feel close without being close?* He leant forward as he spoke, reaching his fists one by one over the table as if pulling me towards him on a length of rope. *Houses should have no doors. Walls separate us.*

Our houses should help us see each other and hear each other and be with each other more!

The next picture showed more cowsheds slotted together. A column of text was squashed in the margins to one side of the page:

*A house is a mach-
ine for living in tog-
ether so our houses
should be smaller to
bring us closer tog-
ether*

The houses are modular, said Touw, *so they're an ideal low-cost housing solution because they can be mass-produced in a factory and assembled on-site.* The first row of cowsheds joined up to form a single-storey circle, to which another row was added, and then another, etc. The sketchbooks showed the rising tower of cowsheds from different perspectives, in plan, in section, from street level, from above. The aerial view showed a void puncturing the core of the building. *What's that hole*, I said. *It's not a hole*, Touw said, *it's a light well.* But it looked like a giant rubbish bin, the kind of place where people would throw their used batteries or empty drinks cartons.

In one image a cowshed had been sliced open to show its interior: a single room, with no dividing walls, furnished with only a built-in bed and a built-in table, both of which, as in a ship's cabin, could be folded up. Beneath the folded-away bed was a toilet, beneath the table was a recessed sink. Touw provided commentary on his diagrams, which were all the time getting progressively smaller and more anatomical-looking, so that I could hardly see without leaning in. *This is a brand new type of hinge*, he said, pointing his chubby fingers at a pair of interlocking loops. *This is a suppressed window-sill*, he said of two offset squares overlaid with a T-shape. *And here* – he identified a pair of bisecting lines – *is a double glass window*. All the while, in the background, the watercolour mountain seemed gradually to be getting less angular, as though somebody had smoothed its edges in sympathy with the tower's rounded geometry. By the end of the notebook the tower must have been thirty or forty storeys high, though it was hard to say exactly because the upper floors were hidden by the clouds, through which the dazzling sun, refracted, stretched its mustard-coloured rays in all directions as if to announce the arrival of a great redeemer.

Chapter 4

Where I am is only
where I am in relation to you and
I'm further from you now than
you are from me

Mim was in the living room, her face framed by the deepening blue of the sky behind her, and I could tell from her expression that she was far away, as if remembering a dream or a passage from a novel. *Where was she?* I looked outside to see what she was seeing – because a window is a pair of glasses that pulls the world into focus – but all I could see was the middle of the tree outside; its canopy severed from the trunk and uppermost leaves.

My old Bechstein had lost a foot on its journey over from London and rocked from side to side as I passed, releasing a mixed-up chord into the room. For several months the piano had been held by customs in some kind of depot and the involuntary outbursts it made as I neared it were the only interaction we'd had since being reunited. The long sea journey had left some nicks and dents in its carapace but it was still a beautiful instrument, one of the last made before the factory was destroyed during the war. It was the piano I'd played since childhood, so at first I'd felt its absence acutely, but rather than missing it more as our separation lengthened, my feelings towards the Bechstein had dulled. So that when a customs official eventually called to say that it risked being sent back to London (I didn't realise I was being asked to offer a bribe) I was not just indifferent but oddly relieved, as though not only had I no desire to play the piano anymore, I wasn't sure I'd ever liked it or wanted to play it at all. And a week later, when the big black instrument was finally hauled up Jacob's Ladder by four straining men, I half-wished for some accident to happen so I wouldn't have to see it or think about it or play it again.

It was late afternoon and the heat of the day was lingering – it was thirty-eight degrees at least – and the air was buzzing with mosquitoes. I was hungry. All I'd eaten for lunch was a gherkin and a piece of leftover steak so old it tasted like liver. I sat down in the chaise, letting the seat slide back under the weight of my body until I was lying down. From the horizontal, the windows framed so perfectly a view of the sky – with no distractions apart from a few branches protruding above the height of the windowsill – that it seemed the window and the chaise might have been designed together for this exact purpose. The sky was clear, an emptiness stretching so far into the distance that I couldn't help wanting to quantify it. I dropped an imaginary tennis ball from the highest point my eyes could imagine and counted the seconds it took to reach the ground. *Ten, nine, eight, seven, six, five, four* . . . But the calculation was inconclusive since it was always possible by straining my eyes a little harder to shift the starting point a little higher.

Something reminded me of an afternoon a few weeks before when, having wandered for an hour or so along the coastal road that wound around the peninsula, Mim and I had discovered a dusty path which led past a few trees to a secluded beach. It was a small beach, not particularly beautiful, but popular with locals, a number of whom were out on such a hot day. There were a few people floating in the sea but really the water was too cold for swimming. We set down our towels and I went to the edge of the surf, wetting my ankles first, then wading in to my knees, then forcing myself deeper, taking a few shallow breaths against the cold.

Afterwards I lay among the other bathers and listened to the low tones of voices around me. I covered my face with my hat. People were sleeping, murmuring, reading. I could hear their rising and falling inflections and could tell when a conversation passed from one person to another from their different vocal qualities and accents, but apart from the occasional exclamation like *What?* or *No!* and the *umph* as somebody stood up or sat down, I couldn't hear what anyone was actually saying. From beneath the rim of my hat, as if in disguise, I scanned the bodies draped in their various degrees of nakedness along the slope leading to the shore. Presently Mim emerged from the water. She was wearing a stretchy black bikini with a sort of Rorschach blot pattern on it. A mother seagull and her chicks who had been pecking at the tideline, retreating each time a wave came in, stood very still as she passed, as if sensing danger, though their eyes were set so far apart that I couldn't tell what they were looking at.

I watched Mim cross the sand and sit down beside me. *Are you sleeping?* she said. And I said, *Yes,* tilting my hat lower to hide my eyes. Her face was blank beneath her thick black fringe and her thick black sunglasses. There was a still expression on her lips. She took off her bikini top, wrung it out, and laid it on the sand beside her. Then she sat for a while unknotting her hair with her fingers before pulling it into a neat, thick, black ponytail. Two women somewhere were talking about finding and curing disease on trees. *It's December!* somebody said. Mim's bikini top must have obscured the size of her breasts because they looked different without it. Beneath her light-brown skin – she had the kind of European skin that doesn't discolour or glisten with sweat – the veins in her chest had gone a very bright blue. I liked looking at her. It wasn't the nudity that attracted me, there was just something about her body which my eye liked, or had at least taken an interest in. And so it was, scanning her figure with a lazy and purposeless kind of attention, that my eyes came across her slightly goofy-looking large brown nipples.

At the exact moment our gaze met, a trickle of water from Mim's ponytail caused the nipples to contract, to crinkle a little, fixing me with such a discomfortingly frank stare that I wanted to look away. I lifted my hat. What was discomforting wasn't the intense way these eyes were fastened on me, it was their indifference, which seemed to *see things* in the way that children seem to *see things* when they stare at you on buses. They were curious about me, yes, but it was a distant and bored sort of curiosity, a sort of scientific curiosity, as if what they were observing was not a known body – the body of someone they knew and loved – but something odd, something that didn't make sense. *What is it?* they seemed to be asking. *Is it a man? Hmmm . . . Let me see.*

Once seen, this second tier of eyes was difficult to unsee. With an almost electric shock I became aware that all around me, below faces hidden by hats or behind books and magazines, these various nipples (the fleshy pink ones, the wayward ones, the stupid-looking ones set too close together, droopy brown aureoles and vulnerable pink ones, the naive-looking mismatched nipples and alert upward-pointing ones, the dopey breasts facing too much to either side) stared unblinkingly from their various chests. *What are you looking at?* I thought. *I'm just lying here! What's so fascinating about that?* But they watched me with such exquisite attention that, like those portraits which seem to follow the viewer with their eyes, it was hard to believe they were interested in anything but me.

Now, lying on the chaise, I couldn't see Mim's face but I could tell from her breathing, which grew softer, that she'd turned away. The church bells rang twice in the bay. Perhaps I'd been asleep because I felt dizzy, as if I were both floating above the chaise and pressing so deeply into it that I might sink through the leather into the shadows beneath. My muscles felt weak and when

I tried to stand, the chaise held me in such a way – with humps under the back and knees – that, like an infant who hasn't yet the strength or coordination to manoeuvre its body, it was hard to leverage myself up. I must have drifted off again because the next thing I knew the church bells were ringing three times in the bay and when I opened my eyes Mim was standing at the foot of the chaise. She was wearing a jacket. I opened my mouth to say something – *Where are you going?* I wanted to say, because a person in a jacket is always going somewhere – but my lips wouldn't move. It was as though my mind and body had become separated in the moment of transition to consciousness, before the body has woken up. Mim leant down and kissed me – it was a short kiss, not long enough to develop into the promise of anything else. She didn't open her mouth or relax her lips to expose their wet underside. *When you kiss someone platonically*, said Hannah Kallenbach, *you use the outside of your lips, and when you love them sexually you use the inside.* Then I fell asleep again and when I woke a third time it seemed that time was reversing itself because the church bells rang twice in the bay. A knocking was coming from somewhere in the house and it occurred to me for a moment that somebody was at the front door, but it was just the empty wooden cur-

tain hooks rattling on the rail. *Where's Mim?* I said –
who was I asking? God? The universe? – and God or
the universe, or Hannah Kallenbach perhaps, replied,
She's gone to the shops to buy you a birthday present.
Which was nonsense, of course, because it wasn't my
birthday. And anyway, what kind of shops are open in
the middle of the night?

AUTUMN

Chapter 5

The capacity to love

Autumn arrived with a general spray of autumn colour. It wasn't winter yet, but it would be; there was a hint in the air of the cold to follow. The village was quiet. The cafes had covered their tables and upturned their chairs and the ice cream shop had its roller shutters pulled shut. Waiters at the fish and chip shop loitered around with nobody to serve. The holidaymakers who'd swarmed the bead shops and art galleries (*I'm looking for a painting with ochre in it, something to go with my Indian silk curtains*) had covered their sofas, locked their houses and left.

I hadn't liked the holidaymakers. I hadn't liked the way they clogged up the roads with their expensive cars and sat around in cafes – the men in cricket hats and the women with their hair curled under – staring at the sea over the tops of their newspapers with their mouths open as though they were so at ease with themselves that they'd forgotten they were in public. All summer I'd longed for them to be gone but when the cavalcade of motorbikes and white sedans towing boats made its way out along the road towards Cape Town, I regretted their leaving. Surrounded by deserted roads and deserted windows, I felt like I'd been separated from the total mass of the population, like someone left in an environment that wasn't intended for humans anymore.

I thought of Mim, but not often. I missed her, but in an ordinary way. I didn't pine for her. I didn't miss her in the way you're meant to miss someone you love. And the truth is that sometimes I even enjoyed the small, unforeseen pleasures of my situation. Like the quiet, or the predictability of days spent alone, or being able to walk around the house naked without it seeming sexual. But there were times in bed, when my feet couldn't find hers to warm themselves against, when all at once my body would register her absence with such shock that I'd go to the window and stare at the empty parking space where her car used to be as though its return were somehow more likely if my gaze was there, waiting for it.

Sometimes, in the afternoons, which were a lonely time, I'd go down to the cafe. Sitting among the families eating and couples fighting and friends meeting for coffee, I'd find myself thinking, though not explicitly, about myself. Or rather, thinking about myself in relation to them. *They are so much better than me*, I'd be thinking. Because as I watched people eating and talking and letting their knees touch under the table, the banal phenomena that are repeated in almost exactly the same way by hundreds of people day in, day out, I was, all the time, making comparisons between myself and them. I watched how long it took people to eat compared to me and thought, *What's the matter with me, why am I so hungry?* I watched people adjusting their hair with their hands and thought, *How often do they touch their hair compared to me?* I watched friends exchanging platitudes and thought, *How bored they look, sitting there. Do they like being together? Why do they choose to spend time with each other rather than being alone?* I watched mothers feeding their children and answering their childish questions and thought, *What is it about having children that gives people pleasure?* Perhaps they liked teaching them things. Then I saw a boy touching his mother's face and playing with her hair and thought, *It must be nice to be adored in that way.*

One afternoon, encircled by strange thoughts like these, I left the house. Instead of taking the coastal road into the village, I made my way along the dirt path that led through the nature reserve on the mountain. The trail was easy and popular with tourists; in summer it was overrun with rosy-faced holidaymakers in hiking gear, but that afternoon, although the cold and the winds had not yet set in, the car park had only the odd car in it, and the path itself was empty apart from a few people shuffling around in raincoats.

The path started out in the direction of the village but it soon became apparent that it didn't lead towards it, or if it did, it did so indirectly, circling towards its destination via a series of staircases and diversions. I walked slowly. All around me – the end of the day was looming – was white grass yellowing, green grass lightening to a yellower, more luminous green. Birds, invisible in some tree, were squawking. I was alert to people passing. I saw joggers and women walking in pairs, their shadows mingling with mine on the path. I saw rock rabbits. I saw a picture of a lost dog sellotaped to a tree and this, for some reason, seemed significant. Leathery shrubs with pale-pink flowers poked from the rock face.

After meandering for an hour or so along the side of the mountain, the path dipped through a forest. It climbed for a while upwards, over some rockier terrain, and then the trail branched. The arrow pointing downwards read CABLE CAR and the one pointing up read HARBOUR. Above me the cable car building stood out grandly against the emptiness of the sky. There were no birds or aeroplanes, just air thickening into dense grey clouds. The light was changing. I stopped, looking down on the bay. Perhaps the choice of route had gotten confused with some more significant decision in my mind because I stood there for some time looking upwards and then downwards and then upwards again. Who knows how long I'd have gone on standing there had not a group of teenagers suddenly appeared. They were smoking and I felt afraid to be alone, with nobody to know that I was gone, no one waiting for me. One of the boys spoke to me in a language I didn't understand, though I could tell from his rising inflections that he wanted something. *No*, I said. He spoke again and again I said, *No*. Then, because they chose the higher path, I took the lower.

The path started off down the slope but turned back on itself after a few minutes before narrowing and entering a ravine so encroached upon by overgrown bushes and trees that it felt less like a path than a tunnel. The sun was setting in earnest now. Something about the time of day and the time of year – like hinges between day and night and summer and autumn – seemed to unhinge me too. I knew where I was but at the same time I had only a vague sense of where I was. Beneath me some amalgam of the failing light and humidity had dematerialised the sea, turning it and the sky into a single grey mass. The rocks, which earlier had been too bright to look at without squinting, grew formless. Shadows came alive with small animals diving away into other shadows. As the light gave way, objects slipped their boundaries and as they did my thoughts blurred, as though seeing and thinking were connected, so that not being able to see clearly meant not being able to think clearly either. I began to make out, I thought, a shape on the path. It looked like somebody walking ahead of me but it was just a long black strip, so it was hard to tell whether they were coming closer from somewhere very distant or the opposite, if they were almost almost gone. My heart sped up because although it wasn't Mim – *of course not* – in the dark, when a person is reduced to the shape of their hair or the colours they usually wear, figures are just figures, and every upright figure could be the person you long for and have been hoping to see.

I walked quickly, following the walker, trusting him or her to lead me somewhere, and before long, hemmed in on either side by black shrubs and black rocks and black foliage, I lost my bearings on the narrow turning path. Once, as a child, my parents had taken me to the Duomo in Milan. Having paid a few lira, we joined the crowds climbing the long spiral staircase to the roof of the cathedral, which offered panoramic views of the city. I remember the sign outside the cathedral as having read FROM THE HIGHEST LOVE COMES THE MOST SHATTERING BLISS, though I suppose it couldn't really have said that. The stairwell was dark and narrow and ascended in a gently sloping spiral; the only light was the light coming in from the slitted embrasures cut into the thick stone wall. I could see only the two or three steps directly ahead of me and the windows were so far above eye level that it was impossible to gauge, in relation to the outside world, how far I'd climbed. The cathedral had looked stumpy from outside but must have been quite tall because I seemed to be climbing endlessly and became so dizzy and claustrophobic from going round in circles that at one point I tried to turn around, but the stairwell was too narrow to squeeze back past the queue of people behind me, so I kept climbing, feeling with each turning step that I was becoming more submerged, more cut off from the world, as though the further up I climbed the further inwards I was going, as if with each stair I was moving deeper into my own body or the maze of my mind.

The mountain path was still lined on either side by a combination of trees and some kind of dense mountain hedge. From time to time I stopped and looked around but all I could see in the dim light were differentiated shades of black and, occasionally, through what must have been a gap in the leaves, the flecked edges of the sea. The path rose higher along the side of the mountain then levelled out, its contours dissolving into the ridge which dropped off sharply beneath me. The air was blood temperature. A cloud of mosquitoes hovered around me and I, because all my attention was on where next to place my feet, let myself be eaten. I had the impression, as if in a dream, that somewhere nearby a dog was driving a few cattle up the mountain.

The stars had disappeared so completely behind the clouds that I didn't see the little cottage until it was right in front of me. It was a plain rectangular building, painted black or built from very dark brown timber, like a fisherman's cottage. Its lights, if it had any, were off, so that like everything else, it was swallowed into the general darkness. The cottage had two doors, a wooden inner door and a netted screen to stop insects, which bounced shut behind me. As the clouds shifted, a strip of dust was illuminated by a beam of moonlight cutting through the room. There were some furnishings inside but not enough to live by: a dining chair but no table, a television but no sofa. Baboons must have ransacked the cupboards because bits of broken glass and half-eaten food were trodden into the floor. On the counter was an aubergine so misshapen it must have been months old. I thought of a story in the *False Bay Echo* about an old lady, *Mrs So-and-So from Capri Road*, who'd been at home one night, tending to her fire, when two men broke in. They tied her hands with the toaster cord and removed her jewellery. *Don't make a fuss*, they told her, *or we'll cut off your head – swish – with a knife*. They took whatever they could, including her furniture. She relaxed her finger so they could take off her wedding ring. *They took it gently*, she said, *like it was made of glass. They took it so carefully that I felt no panic. In fact, I felt so calm, lying there on the carpet, that I was tempted to just stay there and go to sleep in front of the fire.*

I was relieved, shortly after leaving the cottage, to encounter an elderly German hiker who directed me back down the mountain. The path terminated not at the car park but on a stretch of pavement beside the sea. Ahead of me, across the bay, I saw the village. Sounds drifted across the water, the sounds of dishwashers and kitchen porters singing and clapping their hands as they cleaned plates. How wonderful their singing sounded. It presented something to get closer to. It gave a shape to a journey that, until then, had seemed endless. As I walked I tried to sing – and why not, there was nobody to hear me – but my voice seemed to be far down in my chest and when I opened my mouth all that came out was a kind of barking sound, as though I was trying to cough up something that wouldn't come.

The tide was low. Gulls turned in slow arcs overhead. Fishermen came off their boats with their trousers rolled up. *Yellowtail! Yellowtail! Yellowtail! Yellowtail!* they said as they offloaded their catch onto their tarpaulins. I watched a fisherman trap a fish beneath his foot and cut a half moon under its mouth. *Rosie*, he said, throwing the innards into the sea, *come and get your dinner*. A seal who'd been floating in the water with her chest upturned flopped over and swam to the pier. She climbed out and came right up to him, taking the fish and slapping her fins together as if to say *thank you*. *Now, Rosie*, said the fisherman, *you must go and share with your family*. Which she did, letting the fish loose in the water for the cubs, who crowded round snatching bits of flesh.

A yellow-haired waiter standing outside the cafe

smiled at me so genuinely as I passed, his whole face lighting up, that I couldn't help going in. People were talking and laughing. In the kitchen a chef tossed a skillet over an open flame. Barmen unpacked boxes of wine piled onto the black-and-white chequered floor. I thought of Mim and put myself down on whatever chair was nearest. Where was she? I tried to picture her somewhere (because a person who actually exists must *be somewhere*) but since all I knew for certain was that she'd driven off, the only image I could conjure up was a picture of her sitting in the car. *I ought to telephone her*, I thought, *so she's not so lonely*. All the muscles in my legs were tense, as though suspecting the chair beneath me might be about to collapse.

The yellow-haired waiter put down a basket of bread rolls and some butter that had been out of the fridge for some time. *What can I do for you, my love?* he said, and it was just a turn of phrase of course, but I blushed because all at once I had the idea that I would like to be loved, or if not loved then at least liked by him. *No more mussels*, he said. *No more mussels, no more kidneys.* How can you tell if someone would like to be loved by you? Who knows. But maybe! He wore rough cotton trousers with a drawstring waist and a shirt woven from a thread so fine you could see right through to his chest.

The menu was stuck to the remains of someone's spilt drink. *Are you hungry?* he asked, and I suppose I was because there was a pain in my stomach, which is where Mim's absence had located itself, in my empty stomach with no food to temper it.

Two overweight women eating at a nearby table looked up. They seemed to be looking at me but were in fact looking at the wall behind me, which served as a makeshift gallery for local artists. The painting which interested them was on the top right-hand corner of the wall, a faux-religious image of a modern-day Mary and Joseph kissing on a rugged outcrop of rocks in front of the sea. Mary and Joseph were kissing passionately, as though in the process of being separated or reunited (you could tell they were holy from the glow around their heads), but the fact that the rocks they were standing on looked like sirloin steaks undermined any sexual feeling. The overlap of their kissing faces, painted in a flat, almost cubist style, merged into the illusion of a third face that was wonky and dislocated.

Beneath the picture of Mary and Joseph were several portraits which I thought at first were of a number of women with a physical likeness – all large and bald – but in fact all depicted the same woman, just in different painterly styles and poses, sometimes clothed, sometimes naked, sometimes smoking a cigarette, etc. Something about the painter's attention – a mixture of cruelty and curiosity – was strangely titillating and I couldn't help wondering who she was and why the painter had painted her over and over again. The exquisitely intimate nature of his gaze invited one to fantasise a narrative for their situation: A man paints a woman. While he paints she looks at him looking at her. He paints her again and again, not because he finds her sexually attractive (she is, after all, a very large and totally hairless woman) but because he likes being looked at in that way. Seen in this way, the act of painting was a kind of seduction, not an erotic seduction (though sometimes she seems to be looking seductively at him from the canvas) but a sort of visual intercourse, the painter's way of keeping them alone together in the room. There was something disturbing about the portraits. Travelling across the row of paintings, I kept hoping that something would change, that the intensity of the painter's gaze would lessen, that his desire to paint, like the paint itself, would eventually run out. But he seemed to want to go on painting her forever.

Across from me was a man with brown stains on his fingers who was sitting alone. *Excuse me*, he said to the waiter. His accent was thick and he spoke with some difficulty, as if he'd had a stroke. *Excuse me*, he said again. *Can my dog come in?* He pointed outside to a tied-up dog licking itself on the pavement. The dog looked up as if knowing it was being discussed. *It depends*, said the waiter. *Is it the kind of dog that just sits under the table? What kind of dog is that*, the man said, *a dog that's under sedation?* The dog was small and had a stump instead of a tail. It looked happy, happy but with no tail to wag. *I like dogs*, said the waiter, *but I prefer the ones with short hair. A dog is a reason to have conversations with people*, the man said. *About the dog, and beyond.* Then the dog came in and it didn't cause any trouble.

Outside, a family of seals was sleeping on the rocks. The waiter delivered a portion of squid to a group of people sitting nearby. *Mmm*, a man said, *it's so tender. How do you get it so tender?* The waiter said they tenderised it by beating it to death against the rocks. *Ouch!* the man said. *Do they cry? How do squids cry?* the waiter replied. Through the window, boats were sailing in and out of the bay, little boats sailing in behind the big trawlers, as if dragged in their wake. A swarm of seagulls followed the boats, trailing the scent of fish, their white underbellies flashing in the moonlight. The waiter arrived with my food and said, *It's beautiful, isn't it?*

I love rocks, they're so peaceful. He put his hand on the back of my chair and poured me a glass of pinotage. He was *a connoisseur of pinotage*, he said. As I swirled the wine in my glass he noticed my wrist, cocked at an unusual angle. *What happened?* he said. *Nothing*, I said. *Nothing serious. Is it painful?* he asked. *It looks painful. Perhaps a glass of wine will make you feel better.* I looked at the moon, the fast-moving clouds, the moonlight on the water. *Nobody cares about one's personal trials and griefs*, I thought. *One's trials and griefs are boring.*

But actually, at that very moment, the two women eating nearby – Flo and Dot – were having a miserable conversation that was deeply interesting. Flo was fleshy and had a necklace tan. Dot looked like a librarian and had a bun that wanted to come undone. It appeared that Flo had lent money to Dot, who didn't have the money to repay her. Dot's lips were drawn in a line over her teeth as if to stop whatever she had to say from spilling out. Flo was philosophical. *Don't worry about the money*, she said, *the money will come.* But Dot was saying, *I'm sorry, I'm sorry, I'm sorry, I'm sorry* and gripping the menu as though the pressure of her fingers was holding everything together. *What are you sorry about?* Flo said. *What do you have to feel sorry for? Everything will be OK in the end.* They'd been drinking all night, so when the music changed it didn't take much encouragement for Dot to stand up and start dancing, rocking from side to side, raising one leg and then the other in a sort of gumboot dance. At first I turned away, because dancing embarrassed me, but then, because Dot was such a beautiful dancer – the way her body moved was just so *joyful* – I didn't have it in me not to look. After a while Flo started dancing too but her limbs were awkward and disconnected, like an insect dancing on its hind legs, so that it looked less like a dance and more like a struggle. When the chorus came on – *All that's real and all that matters is love* – Dot opened her arms in the general direction of the restaurant in a gesture which seemed to say, *Come into me. All the folds of my soul are open to you,* then leant over and seemed, although I'm sure I'm wrong about this, to be showing us her ass.

Chapter 6

You see, Touw thought he could divine water

At eight o'clock the next morning I woke to the sound of the chain securing the construction site rattling as it fell to the ground. Then a thudding began which stopped a second later only to resume a minute or so after that. I pulled the duvet over my head but the fabric seemed to amplify the sound rather than muffle it. In any case, the orchestration of banging was so unpredictable – it had no rhythm or sonic organisation at all – that it was impossible to sleep because all I could think about was the thudding; even when it stopped I was just waiting for it to start up again.

I went up to the solarium. For weeks the construction site had been quiet. The surveyors had come and done their surveys and the only other activity was somebody occasionally shifting the digger from one side of the site to the other. But now, when I looked behind the house, as though somebody had come overnight and cut away the mountain with a razor, all that was there was a flat plane with a metal storage container on it. Two men in yellow vests were walking around the site. One made his way along the side closest to the fence with an armful of pegs (long metal sticks folded at one end), pushing their tips into the earth at regular intervals, while the other, following behind, knocked them in with a maul.

Through the smell of construction came the smell of the sea. The sea that morning was a uniform nothingness with a purple-grey hue. Dense grey clouds were rolling in. The voice in my head, Hannah Kallenbach's voice, said, *It wants to be a storm.* But for me the clouds held no more shape than a dream. What can a man say about a cloud without sounding like a fool? The dried-up herbs in the planter looked grey. When the sun withdrew behind the clouds, my old white T-shirt looked grey and the concrete slabs lying by the side of the road looked doubly grey. The man with the maul, who gazed up from time to time, his eyes sunk into their deep grey sockets, at the length of land still to be pegged, looked like a character from a Cold War film. Grey trees. Grey trees and houses. All around, as the clouds moved, one species of grey gave way to another. It dulled things, yet the overall effect was not dull. It was compelling somehow to sit there, just registering these shifts. The weight of the clouds didn't dilute the light. Quite the opposite, it distilled it. Since although the light – that of it which emerged through the thick canopy of clouds – had lost its brightness, it had, at the same time, acquired an intensity and restraint, as if in struggling through the clouds it had acquired something of their density.

The man with the maul had taken off his vest and the sea haze made the edges of his body waver as in a mirage. I watched him the way the holidaymakers watched the sea: pruriently, letting my face slacken. Perhaps the earth had been compacted by the diggers because sometimes he had to bring the maul down on a peg several times before the soil gave up and let it in. There was, I thought, something humiliating about the business of hitting in pegs, something about the way the pegs just stood there, waiting to be hit in. Or how the man with the maul said, *Stand still so I can hit you* when he hit a peg at a bad angle and it shied away from him.

Above me the sun flickered through the clouds as though its filament was about to wear out. I left the solarium and entered the living room, causing my old Bechstein to rock and let out its confused imploring sound.

The piano, I had always thought, was the simpleton of the musical world, sounding off at the slightest provocation. Not like the oboe or clarinet, which strained just to produce a note. Nevertheless, I sat down and opened a score by some dull composer, Czerny probably, and started playing. The piano had developed an echo on the high notes which lingered in the air, and I hadn't played for so long that my fingers felt arthritic, moving along the keys in a stiff and lifeless way, an impression heightened by my wrist, which hovered so awkwardly over the keys that it seemed to me the broken bones must have been fused back together at an incorrect angle. It was cold. I stopped playing to adjust the radiator then sat down again. Several times I stood up to fetch a blanket or adjust the piano stool or straighten the leg of my pyjama trousers (which always bunched awkwardly beneath me), then sat down again only to find myself standing up a moment later to make some or other minor shift in my environment. This compulsive getting-up-and-sitting-down continued for some time until, unable to make myself comfortable, I closed the lid and went back to the solarium. The men in yellow vests were still snaking their way up and down the site with their pegs. They worked together. When a row of pegs had been knocked in, the man with the maul came along with a ball of green twine which he attached to the tops of the pegs to create a long green line. First they rationalised the site into a series of green lines. Then, beginning from a northerly direction, they created a series of perpendicular green lines which crossed the original lines at right angles. It became apparent, as the process of unravelling the twine advanced, that they were dividing the site into a grid. The coordinates, I imagined, for some as yet non-existent underground activity – the gas lines, perhaps, or the sewage system.

Later in the afternoon, as the sun was dropping behind the mountain, I returned to the piano, angled the task light down, covered my legs with the blanket and tried again. In the dusky light the notes wavered on the stave. My playing was accompanied by the regular beat of the builders hitting in pegs, though from inside the house the sound was distant and detached, and more defeated somehow. When I stopped to listen to it, it seemed to me that what I heard was not a thud so much as a low ticking sound, as if the old wooden metronome that had accompanied my boyhood practice sessions had returned now to restrain me from getting carried away. The memory of those long and lonely afternoons spent holed up in a practice room with that implacable tick made my heart strain. *It isn't natural to be shut up like that with just a piano for company*, Hannah Kallenbach said. To pass the time I'd tape a sheet of paper over the door window and masturbate, so that to this day the act of masturbation and metronomes are indelibly connected in my mind. *It takes its toll on someone*, said Hannah Kallenbach, *to be alone like that for hours, months, years . . . It makes sense that a person who has spent so much time alone in a room, over time, would come to believe that a room could give him nothing but solitude.*

It took all afternoon for the grid to be fully realised and at the end of the day Touw arrived. He stood to one side, leaning against the fence with his arms crossed. The site looked like it had been covered by a mesh or a loose green weave. He drank a can of something and smashed his boot against a block of paving with an expression of deep concentration. After a few minutes of doing this he crouched down and exclaimed, *Here, I can feel it. I feel the pull of the paranormal. There's a river here*, he called to the workmen. *What should we do with it?* Suddenly I brushed up against a forgotten dream. There was a pause between recalling the existence of the dream and recovering its contents. The dream concerned Hannah Kallenbach, though it was not Hannah Kallenbach herself who formed the subject of the dream so much as the room at the back of her house. I'd dreamt I was walking towards the yellow room along a corridor, only the corridor, with a dreamlike disrespect for proportion, had grown so long (like the corridors in the Houses of Parliament with countless doors opening off either side) that I knew I would never reach it. There seemed, in fact, to be a number of interconnected dreams about the yellow room, or rather its absence. In one dream I reached the door only to find the wood so swollen and the handle so stiff that it wouldn't open. In another I forced the door open only to find the room behind it completely unrecognisable, its walls clad in oppressive wood panels and lined with fax machines and TVs all tuned in to different channels, like some kind of broadcasting station.

Outside, someone shouted and a car door closed with a deep thud. The chain on the gate rattled as the builders locked up to go home. I sat down on the chaise. The temperature was dropping – it was colder than it had been at one o'clock or two o'clock – and the radiator just hummed and whined and issued a damp stream of air into the room. The coldness tired me. Although perhaps it wasn't the coldness that tired me so much as the house, since there is an idea that a house should afford some protection from the weather, yet to me being in the house seemed no different from being out in the world. *If you want to sleep*, Hannah Kallenbach's voice said, *why then do you not sleep?* I walked to the window instead and stood there with my hands clenched. An icy breeze came and went along the skin of my leg as though through a tear in my pyjama trousers. *What is there for me to do but go to bed?* I thought. After all, I had no job, no wife, no child to take care of. *Nothing*, said Hannah Kallenbach. *Absolutely nothing.*

All the while, the worm of cold air disappeared and reappeared on my skin, sending my hand chasing after it in some complicated kind of foreplay. Having felt with one hand along the seam of my pyjama trousers, searching for a hole, I now ran my hand along the window's edge. The sea air corroded things – it had eaten away taps and wires, pipes and light fittings – so perhaps a gap somewhere was letting in cold air. The paint flaked as I touched it. *Where are you?* I said to the hole. *Where are you, if anywhere at all?* Because the window appeared to have no metal frame, merging seamlessly into the concrete around it.

But then, beneath the left-hand corner of the glass, I felt an almost indiscernible groove in the concrete. Like the dink in the head of a very small screw. Was it a screw? It looked like a screw head but it was hard to see because it was covered over with paint. *Why don't you just unscrew it and see what happens?* Hannah Kallenbach said. So I fetched a carving knife from the kitchen. The screw was stiff, so firmly sealed over with paint that it bent back the top of the knife. But, beneath another knife, it gave way. It brought me great pleasure to be *doing something*, to be using my hands again, and I lifted the screw from the wall until it came out completely, leaving a dark tunnel in its wake. Through the tunnel came a jet of cool air. It occurred to me that since a screw is always attached to something, unscrewing it must be severing something from something else, but the activity was so completely engaging that I couldn't stop going over the window with my hands for more screws, and having found them (there were half a dozen or so spaced at regular intervals) unscrewing them. At the end of the row I pressed my hand against the glass, expecting it to collapse in a heap, but it didn't. It must, I thought, have been held in place by some hidden mechanism, or limescale perhaps. In the failing light the window had become a mirror in which I saw a composition of stripes: the crumpled brown stripes of my pyjamas against the black stripe of the piano against the white stripe of the ceiling from which two strips of wire protruded from the remains of a broken light fitting.

That night I felt so lonely that I couldn't sleep. I

soothed myself by imagining I was a child again, at a time in one's life when sleeping alone is not yet lonely. When eventually I drifted off I dreamt of Hannah Kallenbach's yellow room again. But this time when I opened the door at the far end of the corridor, the room I arrived in was not the yellow room but the bedroom I'd slept in as a child, only the things inside it weren't my childhood things but adult things, official-looking papers and books, ceramic pots, a pair of thick-soled sandals. Whereas the other dreams had been vignettes – at least it seemed that way to me, since I remembered only fragments – this particular dream stuck in my mind because it was long and exquisitely detailed. I was sitting on the bed in this room that was either the yellow room or my childhood bedroom or both, when someone knocked on the door. As the door opened I made out the face of Hannah Kallenbach. She stood for a moment, silhouetted in the crack of the doorway. She looked nice, standing there. In the subdued dream light her wrinkles softened. Then she smiled at me with genuine pleasure and said, *What are you doing?* and all at once, from behind her, water came rushing in, swirling around her feet in little eddies. *What have you done?* she was saying now, her voice louder. I saw that she was wearing a coat and some kind of hat. *I'm sorry*, I said.

I'm sorry. Because I remembered that I'd been running a bath upstairs but once the tap had been opened I couldn't get it shut. Hannah Kallenbach was walking towards me with eyes narrowed and her arms crossed so hard over her chest that her breasts were flat. I didn't know what was going to happen but whatever it was aroused a feeling in me that wasn't sexual exactly, but since it was everywhere in my body, I felt it there too. When she reached the bed Hannah Kallenbach leant down and pulled me towards her. *What are you doing?* I said. And she said, *I love you.* But I knew I was dreaming. So I said, *I don't believe you. Tell me again in the morning.*

Chapter 7

Whatever you love most dearly

We'd been warned of high winds and now they arrived, starting with a coordinated movement of leaves in the trees and a slapping of branches on the windows. The wind flew through the house, blowing curtains, rattling door handles, skewing pictures, causing the telephone – which hadn't rung for weeks – to tremble in its cradle. It pushed at the living-room window, which shook and shuddered and then, with one great gust, came out completely.

Blow, blow, blow, said Hannah Kallenbach, whose voice had become the dark background of my days. Avoiding the broken glass, I crossed the room. The empty window made me feel vulnerable in a way that was not entirely unpleasant. How can I explain it?

Through it the tall Gothic spires of the church in the bay looked more exotic somehow. The absence of glass produced a sort of heightened receptivity in me. It made me more susceptible to the world, letting me receive its imprint directly onto myself, like a photographic negative. Through the glassless window, the purple sunrise with its dishevelled horizon seemed grander, and more powerful. Everything was exactly the same as it always had been, of course it was, but there was something vague about the way my eyes registered the world. Whereas previously I could see things clearly – the trees, even their individual leaves – now when I looked out the low-flying gulls were almost indistinguishable from the white specks that came off the tops of the waves. Things were on the cusp of not being themselves. I had the idea that it wasn't my vision deteriorating but the very glue which held the objects of the world together growing old and weak.

When the wind picked up, it moved things, and when it withdrew, everything went still. It blurred the distinction between what was alive and what was not *dead* exactly, but . . . Well, between what had life and what didn't. That was the problem. Or rather, what enlivens things? Does it come from inside or outside? The wind blew thoughts into my head: wild, inappropriate, dreamlike thoughts. When my eyes landed on the row of agapanthus under the house, the plants gazing up at me with their big heads from the flowerbed looked animate. I didn't see plants staring up at me but sentient beings whose tall stalks, depending on their uprightness or the angle of their heads, had a certain humanness. And although I knew that it was sad to attribute to flowers a character they didn't possess, that it was sad to find an animus in plants when all a plant is capable of is processing light, I couldn't help feeling that the tall flower nodding on its stalk was strong yet somehow benevolent, while the skew bloom beside it rising from its leafy body had an affect that was at once quizzical and superior.

Next door, the builders had arrived and were moving around the site tidying things, motioning for each other to come and see this or that bit of damage. Tarpaulins and sheets of chipboard were scattered around the site, not messily so much as in the positions that things might adopt over time to make themselves more comfortable. The tower itself, which by now was well underway, seemed undamaged by the various weathers. The gas lines, which men with picks and shovels had laid the previous week, were intact. So too were the sewers and the foundations. Only the mesh fence between the house and site had collapsed, a fence post ripped right out of the ground with earth still clinging to its foundations. Touw, who'd arrived in his usual orange handyman trousers, was standing at the fallen-down fence with one foot resting on the fence post.

I went around the living room righting pictures and sweeping up the glass and dead leaves that had blown in through the window. Several heavy-bodied spiders had relocated themselves from the garden into the corners of the ceiling. *What a mess!* I said to myself as I went around tidying things. *What a mess.* The dirt around me raised a wave of disgust so powerful that no sooner had I finished the living room than I started on the kitchen, emptying the fridge and washing the forgotten cups of tea which had been piled up in the sink since Mim left. *What a mess, what a mess.* I scrubbed the counter with steel wool until the yellow grime had come away from the grouting and the tiles had returned to their original clinical grey-green.

I made my way down the ramp to rake up the leaves and branches that had blown down from the mountain. But in the entrance hall I stopped and looked back towards the laundry. Halfway down the corridor was the washbasin. *To wash off the outside world*, the South African academic had told me. And at first I'd liked that, the idea of cleansing oneself of the outside world. After all, wasn't that what I'd come for? To be *cleansed* of something? But this was the first time I'd actually used it and I scrubbed myself thoroughly, almost angrily, feeling it necessary to really clean myself. *What are you doing?* said Hannah Kallenbach. *I'm cleaning out*, I said. But *cleaning out* wasn't right. *Cleaning out* was how South Africans described a certain kind of burglary. Someone has been *cleaned out*, they'd say, when the burglars had taken absolutely everything. I was *flushing out*, then.

Past the washbasin, at the end of the corridor, the door was closed. I'd avoided the laundry since Mim left. It was a lonely room, such a lonely room that just the idea of it was hateful. But that morning something felt different. I made my way past the basin, down the corridor, and, having opened the door, stood for a while in the doorway with my heart beating so hard it lifted the fabric of my pyjama shirt. It was a bright day but down there the air was thick, a damp grey haze. Unlike the first floor, which was raised off the ground on pillars, the rear section of the ground floor had been excavated from the rock behind it – scooped out of the mountain, you might say – which made it cavelike, especially now, when its window was almost completely covered over with ivy. The light was gone and in the dim light – it was half or almost completely dark – it was hard to make out the dimensions of the room, or where the walls met the ceiling.

Mim's things were scattered around the room. Beside the door were shoes, at least ten pairs. *What a mess*, I thought, staring into the mustiness. Flakes of paint or dust covered every surface. The floor was piled so high with things that the only way to traverse it was by walking on top of them; each time I lowered my foot it raised a cloud of dust. A shrine of sweet wrappers was piled up on a stack of magazines beside a wineglass full of cigarette ends. Mim's raincoat lay on the floor where she'd left it, having long forgotten her shape. Its pocket contained a few coins of too little value to bother with. *What a mess*, I was thinking, but there was something sinister about the arrangement of things across the room, something more than just mess, something unified, as though the objects had not just been strewn around randomly but were shying away from something. *Like the debris from a fallout*, said Hannah Kallenbach. *Yes*, I thought. But when I opened my mouth to say it – *Like the debris from a fallout, exactly!* – it felt like a heavy weight had been dropped onto my sternum and my voice came out squashed and childish. Which was apposite, I suppose, because there *was* a childishness about what I was doing, as if by tidying the room I could return things to how they were, which is of course the worst kind of wish, the wish to reverse something, the wish to say, *I take it back*, or, *I preferred it before.*

On Mim's desk – a concrete slab that must have been designed as an ironing table – was her laptop, its red light flashing in resistance to the room's gloom. When I touched it a half-finished game of solitaire appeared, causing several of the mosquitoes which invaded the house nightly (drawn to its glass windows as to a large lantern) to appear from the shadows, their affections transferred to the bright light of the screen. Beside the computer was a piece of paper. *My dearest Max* was written at the top of the page. *My dearest Max*, it said, nothing else. One side of Mim's note was rough, as if torn from a book. On the other side was a block of printed text, a section of which had been circled in blue ink: *Walls shouldn't be strong, they should be soft and enclosing.*

Then the computer went dead and the room went dark. Groping around among Mim's papers and empty sweet wrappers I found a box of matches. The lit match cast a flickering glow, illuminating a spider suspended directly above me: it was thick and velvety and didn't scurry. I took the flame to the bottom of the web and let it creep up to the spider sitting there, and burn it. For some reason – perhaps the flame had punctured a small hole in its abdomen before melting it completely – the spider began to squeal before disintegrating onto me (and Hannah Kallenbach too, because she was also there).

I rifled through Mim's things looking for the rest of the letter, or other drafts of it. A stack of open books lay beside the computer, face down, as though Mim had stopped reading them halfway through. *Perhaps she was bored of them*, Hannah Kallenbach said. Or the opposite. I imagined Mim in a flurry of ambition, impatient with how long it took to get through a single book, thinking, *Right! I'm going to read them all right now, at the same time*. In the pale light from the corridor, I opened the uppermost book. It was called *The Hidden Messages in Water* and suggested that the shape of water was determined by its relationship to the people around it. There were photographs of water crystals, which, if you looked at them closely, revealed minute differentiations: a glass of water which had been shouted at, said the author, appeared murky under a microscope, while one subjected to declarations of love ran clear. Beneath it was a book called *Aqueous Architecture*, which was not, as I'd expected, about buildings with sea views or water features (like Frank Lloyd Wright's Fallingwater, which has a river running through it) but about how water changed the structure of consciousness. If *The Hidden Messages in Water* believed that human consciousness changed the structure of water, then *Aqueous Architecture* believed the reverse. The author wasn't interested in buildings made *with* water, it turned out, so much as buildings made *like* water. He listed the various forms water could take: there was water, of course, but also water vapour, and cloud formations. *What is a cloud?* he asked. *What would it be like to live in a fog or a mist?*

But I was paying less attention to the contents of the books than scanning their margins for traces of Mim. Here and there she had struck out a sentence in blue ink or encircled a passage or inserted a question mark or note into the margins. On one dog-eared page she'd underlined the phrase *Buildings should close around a body the way a mother holds a baby.* On another, beside the words *People should enter their houses like a drop of blood entering a puddle of water,* she'd drawn an exclamation mark. I tried, by triangulating the marking to the words it referred to, to decode what she'd been thinking while she was reading, but the circles and exclamation marks meant nothing to me. I tried to gauge by the marks her pen had made what mood the hand making them had been in (a heavy underlining suggesting anger, a messy circle indicating frustration and a desire to move on). But really her marginalia were illegible, less like words or symbols than a long blue thread which had come unravelled somewhere inside Mim and I, now, was trying to reel back in.

At first the laundry had smelled of damp walls but beneath the musty odour I began to detect a second smell, a secretive smell, hidden beneath or rather *within* the first one, because although she'd been gone for some time, Mim's perfume had been preserved in the airless room, only mixed in with the earthy scent of the walls, it'd grown deeper and muskier, more pungent, and so intensely evoked Mim's presence that all at once it made me want to weep. So I sat down and cried, or tried to, because the tears were like grout; I only managed to squeeze a few out with great effort.

Then I came across a memory. It wasn't a distant memory, nor one I'd forgotten. In fact, it was something I'd have thought of often had I not made a strenuous effort to avoid it. The memory was of the afternoon Mim had arrived in South Africa. We were driving away from the airport and I remember that as we passed the large supermarket on the motorway out of Cape Town she turned to me, glassy-eyed, and said, *You know, I really love that child* (she was talking about her sister's newborn son). She said, *I love him in spite of all the reservations I have about children. Maybe it's because I was there just after he was born* (she arrived four or five hours afterwards) *but last night when I said goodbye to him it felt like it was my own child I was leaving. I felt so close to him that it seemed there was no boundary between us, particularly physically, that there was no limit to my affection for him. I mean, of course there's a limit, but . . .* For some reason we were both crying. *What are we crying about?* I said and she laughed a humourless laugh that said, *Life is funny, isn't it?*

Somewhere a dog started barking, causing another dog to bark somewhere else. On and on they went. Continuing my spring clean – which now was just a euphemism for scouring the room for clues about Mim – I came to a small metal filing cabinet. One by one I emptied the drawers, finding receipts, bank statements, a list of ingredients (*polenta chilli anchovy mint*) for a meal I don't remember eating, expensive cufflinks, a silk scarf, French toothpaste, a prescription for medication I didn't recognise, a variety of circulars addressed to *Whomever it concerns*, a picture of me as a boy with a severe side parting, a race-track packet of contraceptive pills (half of which had been popped from their plastic sockets), a stopped watch, a number of spiders the size of ping-pong balls and a letter to Jan Kallenbach from someone who didn't know that he was dead so they couldn't reach him.

The bottom drawer was locked so I knelt down on the floor and forced it open. Inside was a small notebook with a black cover. I hesitated before removing it, then did, but left the room without opening it. *What are you waiting for?* Hannah Kallenbach asked me, and I said, *I don't know.* It wasn't the contents of the notebook which frightened me, it was its secretiveness. It must, I thought, have contained something I didn't want to know, or why would she have kept it in a locked drawer where I wouldn't find it? All evening I carried Mim's notebook around but did nothing with it. At the end of the day, I filled up the blue mosaic bathtub and sat in it, not washing myself, just sitting there with the notebook on my sternum, studying the weeds insinuating themselves through the edges of the skylight. Then, putting it aside, I slid down beneath the surface of the water until my head and shoulders were covered and the sea, from underwater, sounded like a distant volcano.

Chapter 8

The only way to understand the sea is to drop a grid on it

For days I delayed opening the notebook through a series of deferrals. I'd pick it up while brushing my teeth then put it down again so as not to ruin the experience by reading in the bright light of the bathroom. I'd pick it up while waiting for the kettle to boil then put it down again so the squealing wouldn't break the flow of my concentration. I'd bathe for hours and comb my hair in various ways. The more I waited the more afraid I became of the notebook, and the more afraid I became the more I kept it closed, as if by doing so its contents might remain imperceptible or even disappear. But the more I carried it around the heavier it became, until the experience of carrying it had become so embedded in me that it was hard to tell whether it was its weight I was carrying around or mine. At the end of each day I'd lie on the chaise, angle the reading light down, pick up the notebook to read it, then put it down again because, having held it so constantly, my wrist ached.

Each day and into the next, it rained. Through the window the sea swelled and the boats looked small. Grasses slid down the mountain with so much earth attached to their roots that it seemed the mountain itself was disintegrating. There was something primitive about the rain. It made me want to *see* people or *be with* people. It wasn't a calming rain, making uniform watery noises, it was a whipping rain that beat on the skylight and came in sideways through the glassless window. The newspaper showed flooded streets and floating cars. The story of the weather had become the story of the defences people constructed against it. The radio spoke about stocking cupboards with tins. Cartoon characters converted household items into flotation devices (the legs of the dining-room table are removed to become oars, the flat tabletop is a raft).

One day, as the afternoon neared its ending, with a vegetable soup on the stove, and the potatoes far from cooked, I went to the living room to read. I shut the door, sat down, covered myself with a blanket, picked up the notebook and might very well have put it down again when, because the binding was weak, a clump of pages fell out. The outermost page was a blank white expanse with no words for my thoughts or feelings to snag on, and I let my eyes wander up and down it as if at a strip of magnificent coastline. Overleaf were a few lines of Mim's messy scrawl. *Brace yourself*, said Hannah Kallenbach. What was I afraid of? A letter, I suppose. *Dearest Max*, the letter might read, *if you are reading this then I must be dead.*

But the notebook didn't contain notes about Mim, it contained notes about the sea. They weren't written in full sentences but were phrases stacked up on top of each other like a poem. *The sea is infinite, the sea is eternal*, etc., nothing insightful, just the usual generalised observations people make about the sea. I turned the page and found more banal observations. *So this is it*, I thought. *I can see why she hid this away. These are just the nonsense clichés which people have been making about the sea for centuries.*

I thought about the kind of people who come to the sea to look at it, how they put themselves down on whatever rock or bench is around and gaze for hours into the distance as though something out there makes life seem meaningful, or at least less incomprehensible. *What are they looking at?* I asked myself. *What do they see when they see the sea?* Most people seemed to find the sea deeply interesting but it held no particular depth or virtue for me. The most profound effect the sea had on me was that sometimes, from the living-room window, it quite literally made me want to throw up. I'd always thought that people who liked the sea were people who didn't like society, that it was people who'd failed in their relationships who turned to the sea. There was something in their glazed faces – leaning on harbour railings, walking along the crumbling promenade, staring over the tops of their newspapers – which disturbed me. It seemed they wanted to be immersed in it, that as they looked out at the sea they entered into a special relationship with it which, to a certain extent, entitled them to speak to it. Because people who spent too much time looking at the sea did start to commune with it, as if nature held the answer to all of life's important questions, their expressions suggesting that they were not so much watching the sea as conversing with it. I could tell from the way they sat, dead still, that the sea *spoke* to them and that they, for their part, were receptive to its communication. But what was the sea saying to them? The sea didn't speak to me. *What do you say to them that you won't say to me?* I asked the sea, but the sea was silent and had no communication to make.

The sea glints, Mim had written. *The sea seethes.* In this vein were written an extraordinary number of pages. *The sea is lonely* and *The sea is wide* and *The sea looks like the ridges on the palate of a person's mouth. The sea sighs*, she wrote, though it seemed to me that what the sea was really saying, if anything at all, was *why*, or *who*, or *whywhywhy*. It was apparent from the number of pages Mim had written, mottled with traces of her rubbings-out – *the sea shivers*, she'd written, no, *quivers*, no, *shakes* – that she'd watched the sea closely, methodically even, yet as the notebook progressed her notes said less and less about anything, everything just ended up as some metaphor to do with water. Sometimes, despite being neither forensic nor lively enough to be worth repeating, an observation would appear twice – that the sea was like *sequins*, for instance, or *the metallic blue of the BMWs they used to use in road trip movies* – which was disconcerting, breaking, as it did, the promise inherent in reading, that, line by line, as one thing leads to another, one is all the time *going somewhere*, that if one keeps going, one will eventually *get somewhere*, to some end or conclusion.

As the day wore on it became harder to read, not because I didn't like what I read but because the clouds were dark and it was too dim to read without squinting.

An image of Mim floated into my mind, clarifying for a second before it was swallowed up again. Sometimes I'd come into the laundry and find her sitting at the desk, her face whitened by the light from the computer screen. *What are you doing?* I'd ask, and she'd say, *Nothing,* though I could see from the reflection in the window behind her that she was playing solitaire. *What did she see when she looked at the sea,* I wondered. *Perhaps it was just something to look at,* said Hannah Kallenbach, *a convenient place to rest her eyes.* But why did she need to put it into words? It occurred to me that this business of writing things down must have mattered to Mim personally, that in among her thoughts about the sea must be other thoughts; that someone who fixed their eyes for hours and hours on something a thousand miles from nowhere, must find, after a while, that it was their own thoughts they came up against. But the more I read the less I understood, since as the notebook progressed, perhaps because her hand was tired, Mim's handwriting loosened and the words began to lean away from me, as if hiding something. *What are you looking at?* they seemed to say. *We're just words! We don't like being scrutinised in this way!*

The point about the sea, it seemed, was not to look at it but to capture it somehow, to turn it into words the way a painter might fix the sea in variegated shades of blue or a composer might transcribe it into wave-form music. So I went to the window to see for myself. The ocean looked exactly as I had expected it to look: vast and blue and boundless. *What are you doing*, asked Hannah Kallenbach, though being in my head, she must have understood without my having to explain. I scoured its surface for signs of life but apart from the odd seagull there was nothing to be found. I tracked the minute tide movements, trying to decipher the order underlying the fleeting patterns on its surface, which were always changing depending on where you focused your eyes. I opened the notebook and recorded my observations. *Parts of it are clear*, I wrote, *others are scummy. It moves from the pavement to the horizon then back again. Some things get sucked beneath the surface while others stay floating on top of it.* Then, because I didn't know what I was doing, I closed the notebook. *You want to see something*, said Hannah Kallenbach. *You want the sea to show you something and when it doesn't you think it's wasting your time.* So it was that my first attempt to study the sea came to nothing.

Later, because I tried a second and third time, the experience was almost traumatic. My many vague thoughts masked one very clear one: there was simply too much of it. Just the idea of it filled my mind with inconceivably large numbers. In fact, I felt a strong temptation *not* to look at the sea, though I fixed my eyes on it anyway, as if by staring hard enough they might dip down a thousand yards and get to the bottom of whatever mystery lay beneath the gulls and dead leaves. But however hard I tried, I couldn't see what you're meant to see when you look at the sea. So, having dedicated myself for some time to observing the water, I came to the conclusion that nothing I could say about it was insightful.

The rain stopped and I went up to the solarium. The sun came out from behind the clouds (*the sun came out from behind the clouds*, we say, though really it's the clouds that are passing) but the paving had been sunk in water so long that it had lost its hardness and gone soft and almost woodlike. A crab scuttled out from under a flowerpot and darted away. I watched a municipal worker clearing leaves from the railway tracks, jumping back each time a train squeaked past. Fishermen bent over their hooks and tackle, so accustomed to the sea that they paid it no attention. Whereas from the living room the close-up view of the sea made it seem restless and constantly moving, from the solarium, seen in its entirety, it was obvious it wasn't going anywhere. *The sea twitches*, I thought. *Perhaps that's why she watched it, without worrying, not even for an instant, about waking to find it gone from the bay.* I zoomed out, letting my eyes relax until the sea beneath me was just a long blue line which, at a certain point, became the horizon. Nothing stood out. Nothing drew itself to my attention. In fact, the more I looked at the sea, the less I seemed to see it, and this special way of *not looking* produced a feeling in me that I was sort of there and sort of not there, a feeling which lasted for a few minutes until, because it troubled me, I wrote it down – *There are times*, I wrote, *when I'm looking at sea and it's all so dull I can hardly be sure I even exist* – and felt myself again. *I stand here thinking these strange philosophical thoughts*, I wrote, and a sort of happiness came over me, or comfort maybe, as if there were suddenly two of us, as if my writing down my thoughts was a way of keeping myself company.

After half an hour or thereabouts the rain returned, a reprieve doubly cruel for its brevity, since there was neither enough time for the puddles to be reabsorbed into clouds nor for the sun to blast away all my thoughts. When I came downstairs, the phone was ringing. In all the months of living alone, I'd not gotten used to being alone. When the phone rang I couldn't help hoping – just for a second while the caller's identity was still unknown – that it was Mim calling, knowing at the same time that the moment I picked it up the disappointment would make my stomach drop as it does coming over a steep hill. When I picked up the phone, the line was quiet. *Hello?* It was a woman's voice which eventually spoke. *Hello?* it said again because, perhaps since I'd not spoken to anyone for a long time, I'd forgotten to say something. Hannah Kallenbach's voice was warm and soft but loud at the same time, as though amplified by its surroundings, like when someone is calling from a phone box. *Are you OK?* she said. *I just wanted to find out how you were . . . How you are, I mean.* The question gave me a strained feeling: like happiness, or sadness, or both (as if we've two different names for the same feeling), or maybe something else entirely which just shares their intensity. *Oh*, I said, *thank you.* Her voice lowered, taking on the kind of conspiratorial tone that suggests one is about to be let in on a secret. *I was worried that the phones were down*, she said, *so I wouldn't be able to reach you.*

The moment I put the phone down I lost all memory of the conversation. With it went the memory of everything that had happened around it, all of which disappeared the way that, when you wake up, you lose dreams. I tried to orient myself with questions like *What day is it?* or *What was I saying five minutes ago?* or *Who was it I was talking to on the telephone?* but couldn't answer any of my questions so I stopped the test and tried to forget it too. My mind was blank apart from the word *Hannah*, which circled in my head like a trapped insect. *Hannah*. Like Mim, it read the same in both directions. *Hannah, Hannah.* I said it twice, as if to expel it by saying it out loud, then a third time because it was a pleasant sound, enveloping, with no harsh plosives for the tongue to trip over.

That night, although I knew I was alone, I didn't feel that I was alone. When I walked to and fro in the windowless room, the darkness turned the glass wall into a mirror so it looked like there were two of us walking in the room at the same time, the other following me like a double. And when I looked out at the invisible black sea, the lighthouse consoled me by casting its beam across the water, illuminating some gulls floating in the darkness. And later, when it was quiet and the restaurant music no longer echoed through the bay, the sea sound was like someone breathing in the room with me. I lay down and closed my eyes, feeling a clenching in my heart. Shaking my head from side to side, as if to refuse something, or to burrow my way into sleep, I caught myself muttering, *Everything will be OK, everything will be OK in the end*, without knowing why, as if somewhere inside, I knew that being asleep was more dangerous than being awake.

Chapter 9

The sun came out from
behind the clouds, we say,
though really it's the clouds
that are passing

Morning arrived and I opened my eyes, pushing the notebook slowly to one side. It wasn't light yet. I could measure the distance of things by their colour: those nearest were bright and vibrant; those furthest away were grey, as if covered in ash. *It must be Sunday,* I thought, because the building site was quiet. As my eyes adjusted to the dark, I saw Hannah Kallenbach leaning against the radiator, looking down on me with her special piercing gaze. *What are you looking at?* I said. And she said, *I like watching you wake up. I like the way that, for a few moments, you're OK.* Because for a few moments everything was calm and then it began to shake. I thought there might have been an earth tremor, or that a washing machine somewhere was on spin cycle, but the glass of water beside my bed had no ripples on its surface. For a moment (since each night in dreams I reversed Mim's leaving so that in the morning it happened all over again) I had the notion that the bed was moving because Mim was beside me, sobbing maybe, or masturbating. Then I heard the sounds of something dropping, and again the house shook as a crane offloaded a stack of bricks from a van parked on the street into a large metal skip. I couldn't see the crane in its entirety, all I could see was the apex of its bent elbow as it lifted the bricks, swivelled, and released them with a loud crash.

Gradually, the tower had begun to resolve itself into a form I could recognise. On top of the square podium the skeleton of the building had been erected – a dozen or so round floorplates supported by thin columns. There were no outer walls or windows yet, just these evenly spaced floorplates rising up around the large columns for the lift shafts, with staircases zigzagging between them. I could see the stairwells and the corridors, and the rooms leading off them. The electrics had gone in and bits of wiring poked from the where the plug sockets and light switches would be. Touw had arrived on site in a pair of maroon britches and leant a tall ladder against the wall of the apartment tower. He was fitting a bright-green flag onto a flagpole made from a piece of timber. TOUW STUDIO said the flag. MAKING EXTRAORDINARY PROJECTS HAPPEN! The builders, watching as he tightened the rope of the flag around the makeshift flagpole and, turning his hands, fastened it, looked to be experiencing collective bemusement.

All the while, it rained. The sea was flinging up brown sand and lifeguards had raised red flags to keep surfers off the huge waves coming in, each one beginning almost before the previous one was over. In the months since I'd arrived, the building site had been animated by changing noises. In the early days, while the builders were breaking ground, I'd mostly heard loud drilling and jackhammers breaking up rocks. Then had come the peaceful time while the foundations were being laid, which in due course had given way to the construction stage, with contractors arriving on site each morning, each with a different job, making a different sound. Mostly there were delicate sounds – the fine metal sounds of a chain swinging, its links clashing in a metal chord; the even roar of an electric sanding machine – accompanied by the large, generous rumble of a concrete mixer. But sometimes, since I couldn't always see which instrument or tool each sound corresponded to, I had to imagine a machine producing a tired squeal or one which emitted tapping sounds in such a quick rhythm that – in the same way as the multiple notes of a saw's teeth sounding close together are identified simply as 'sawing' or the many incisions of a drill are just called 'drilling' – they merged into a single high-pitched whine. So that during the day, as I lay on the chaise, my thoughts were constantly being infiltrated by odd hypotheses. When, for instance, I heard stones knocking together, I pictured stones being cleaned in a large washing machine, and when I heard a metallic scratching sound, I pictured somebody sweeping the dirt with a metal-bristled broom, and when a faint whirring filled the air, I imagined that someone somewhere was grinding coffee or sharpening a pencil with an old electric pencil sharpener.

What disturbed me, however, was not the mysteriousness of the individual sounds – which, in themselves, were not especially aggravating – but the sounds that the builders (more of whom arrived every day) made working simultaneously. Because although I knew that each of the builders was acting independently, oblivious of the others, I couldn't help searching for some kind of synchronicity between them, as though, like an orchestra tuning up before a performance, their many tools were just warming up for the moment, always imminent, when they would come together into some kind of coherent organisation. My ears, unable to switch off this hope for the resolution the site seemed to be crying out for, were constantly alert for any regularity, believing always that a hammer striking (*one, two, three* – pause – *one, two, three*) might be counting the rest of the instruments into rhythm, or that some sonic coincidence, like the scrape of a spade running for a few seconds in parallel to the grating of a drill, signified something *more*. As though the bricklayer smoothing mortar and the roofer laying flashing and the plumber installing a pipe and the workman transferring gravel from something into something else were, all the time, on the verge of aligning themselves, of synchronising into some form which would reveal the underlying structure according to which the site was arranged.

All day, I listened to the completely unpredictable orchestration of banging with a burning sensation in my chest. The lack of rhythm drove me nearly insane and I couldn't wait for six o'clock when the mechanical sounds gave way to the human sounds of laughing and talking as the builders packed up and went into the corrugated hut to change clothes. But the moment the gate closed and its chain clinked shut, I regretted their departure since my ears, having listened with such attentiveness during the day, couldn't switch off their sensitivity to each sound. Even when the world went quiet, they heard the smallest noise acutely. Especially at night. No sooner had I closed my eyes than my highly attuned ears would detect some sound – the creaking of a ventilator or my foot rubbing against the bed linen – which, like a conductor raising his hand, would draw in some other sounds, and then a whole host of sounds which during the day would have meant nothing to me, but in the dark, when it was hard to link the noise to the object it came from, seemed strange and sinister. However calm I felt when I lay down, within moments of switching off the light, my ear would fixate, for instance, on what sounded like two pieces of wood being knocked together, a sound which seemed so threatening that I'd stay dead still for minutes – hours, even – hardly breathing in case the air squeaking through my blocked sinuses alerted the intruder to my presence. Then the noise stopped. Then it started up again, only this time it seemed less like two pieces of wood knocking together than a thin piece of wood creaking, like a wooden clothes horse being folded away. For a moment I felt relieved – *it was just someone folding laundry*. But of course it couldn't be a clothes horse because why would an intruder be folding a clothes horse, and in any case, I didn't have a clothes horse, I hung the washing over a cable strung between two trees. It was as though the inner membrane of my ear had been worn away. Sometimes I even took the sound of my own breathing for the sound of an intruder's footsteps dragging their way along the corridor towards me. And at those times, above all, I missed Mim. I longed to be able to turn over and know by her unchanged breathing or the calm expression on her sleeping face that whatever rustling or scraping had frightened me didn't worry her, so there was nothing for me to worry about either. *What are you so afraid of?* I'd comfort myself, trying not to respond to every noise that came out of the dark with a paranoid start. *There's nothing to worry about.* But when, in the middle of the night, a sound emerged from the darkness, it was so alarming that I'd jump out of bed, convinced that I was not alone – *those are definitely footsteps!* – and rush to the window only to fasten my eyes onto complete blackness. For a moment I would hear something, a scratching for instance, as though somebody – an archaeologist? – were chiselling away at the mountain, and I'd say, *Hello?*, then, suddenly timid, *Hello?* again, picturing whoever was out there staring back up at me.

Even when I fell asleep my ears, like two sentries guarding me overnight, stayed open. So it would happen sometimes that long after midnight, in the time of deepest sleep, I would wake because someone was calling for me, or not calling *for* me so much as calling out my name with a rising inflection, the way someone hearing a noise when they think they are alone calls out *Hello?* I'd try to ignore the sound – it wasn't Mim, I told myself, *of course not* – and although I knew it was just a dream, I couldn't help believing that it *might be* her, that she *might be* downstairs, standing at the door calling for me, waiting for my reply. Despite myself, I'd lie there, making not the slightest movement, in case she called again, sometimes even responding with my own *Hello?* and lifting my head from the pillow in the hope that something other than the ticking of my watch could be heard on the other side of the room. Then I'd fall asleep again, but too soon, before the dream had been fully blown away by wakefulness, so that sometimes Mim's presence remained and I'd wake again during the night to feel her prodding my shoulder. *I must be snoring*, I'd think, rolling over, but her hand would keep up its prodding until I opened my eyes and found a dark shape standing over me. *What are you doing?* I'd say, and when she didn't reply, I'd try to shush myself back to sleep – *Ssh*, I'd say, *Ssh, ssh, you're dreaming, it's just a dream* – but nothing my eyes told me as they grew accustomed to the dark erased the feeling of dread in my heart.

It rained for days, for weeks, each daily outpouring coming more voluminously from the clouds than the last. The rain had breached the boundaries of the house. It came in through the glassless window of the living room and through the corners of the ceiling where the flat roof was improperly sealed. Damp rose on the walls of the entrance hall where the foundations were too shallowly laid and filtered into the upstairs walls where water had penetrated the facade. The roof had become a breeding ground for mosquitoes. Clouds of them drifted into the living room, where the atmosphere was better for living. They surrounded me so that it felt like I was being tried by a council of mosquitoes – *What is he waiting for?* they said. *He must be waiting for something, something in particular.*

Before long, the tea-coloured stains began to leak and I arranged a number of saucepans under the ceiling so there were now a variety of places around the house which produced a regular rhythm as heavy raindrops fell into the metal pots. The dripping sound had the opposite effect to the unpredictable orchestration of the building site. Where the noises from outside were so irregular that I was constantly being alerted to their presence, the water falling into the pots, tempered as it was by the many layers of roofing and ceiling materials, was so evenly distributed that it had a reliable beat and my mind soon grew accustomed to its presence. The enduringly uniform tempo of the rain dripping into the house provided me with a sense of security. Hearing it, like a baby soothed by a ticking clock, I felt reassured, both of the rhythm's own constancy and of the house's ability to protect me. Since the rhythm, which stood in counterpoint to the chaos outside and the vagaries of the rain (which raged against the skylight, settling into a beat for a moment or two only before the wind changed direction and it became unfamiliar again), distinguished inside from out, giving the impression, so seldom experienced anymore in the house, that *being inside* meant *being separate from the outside world*, so the experience of the rain, from inside, was detached: I could sit there and watch it like a film about rain.

For days the urge to play the piano had found outlet in a constant foot-tapping and teeth-chattering and pressing of fingers against thighs. Now I sat down at the piano. Chopin's *Preludes* fell open, out of habit, on the Raindrop Prelude. The ivory keys were brown around the edges and the fingering pencilled into the score had faded but my hands remembered where to go, the right hand carrying in the melody, the left coming down repeatedly on the A flat which runs throughout the piece. My hands were cold – a luminous, bloodless yellow – and however hard I tried, my left wrist kept collapsing. *The little bird!* I'd remind myself, because my Russian piano teacher had told me to keep my wrist high up as though cradling a bird's egg beneath the palm of my hand, but it was no good, the muscles had atrophied since the accident and didn't have the strength to hold it for very long.

The Raindrop Prelude's recurring A flat, I had always thought, was one of piano playing's greatest paradoxes. The fact that technically it was so easy – with its many repeated notes – made the prelude seem generally more straightforward than, say, pieces with lots of complex finger manoeuvrings. Yet its simplicity was precisely what made it so complicated, because how can a person strike a single note over and over at exactly the same volume and tempo? After all, apart from the physical challenge, since a finger strains when performing the same movement repeatedly, the pianist's problem is to find a way to play the note *with feeling* so that the repetitiveness of a single note heard again and again with absolutely no variation does not become boring.

As is traditional among pianists, I had always alternated between the index and third finger to keep the tempo regular and stop either from becoming overtired. But the scar tissue from the accident, or perhaps the metalwork itself, had stiffened my fingers so the index finger of my left hand came down heavily and loudly on the A flat with a regularity so exact it was almost militant. And whereas previously the left hand had intuitively responded to the melody in the right, making subtle adjustments in volume and tempo and tone to add colour, softening instinctively in the places where the melody was pleading or seductive and vulnerable, now it came down on the A flat with absolute consistency.

That my left hand had acquired this mechanical quality ought to have neutralised the prelude's capacity for misery but instead it brought it to the fore. And as I played automatically, like some kind of pianola, my mind thought about other things, thoughts unrelated to the music, thoughts about Mim, for instance, and my childhood piano lessons. I remembered the two grand pianos my Russian piano teacher had kept side by side in her converted garage, a black Yamaha for everyday playing and a Steinway for special occasions and Shostakovich, and how if I arrived early I stood outside to listen to the breathy *puh-puh-puh* of her keeping time. Sometimes, if I stood on my toes to reach my eyes over the glass, I'd see her leaning forward, her pockmarked face elongated and sheared in two by the swirled brown windowpane so that her long dark hair bled into the piano as though she was not so much playing it as being sucked in by it.

What do you like so much about this piece? said Hannah Kallenbach. Because although the fingers of my left hand felt detached, like a set of nerves which had come apart from the rest of the neural system, my eyes had closed and I'd tilted over the piano as you do when you're about to fall over. *I can't explain it,* I said. It wasn't the narrative of Chopin's illness or the rain that moved me, it was the way my hands moved in relation to each other. They seemed to understand something about the piece that I had never understood myself. Before, they had been a pair, operating together, but now they were independent. Previously, in the opening bars, my left hand, responding to the right hand's tentative melody, had softened and slightly slowed its repeated A flat to echo it, but now, with its pins and its fused joints, it ignored it and just kept on striking its key as firmly and evenly as a pulse. And a few bars on, as the rain swelled and the melody became dejected, whereas previously the left hand had elongated its A flat in sympathy with the melody, now its note remained unswayed. That night, as I sat at the piano, the piece wasn't just a retelling of the story of Chopin and his situation (like mine, only more lonely), it was something that was happening, there on the piano, a relationship unfolding between two hands which were like two characters, one expressive, the other inexcitable, who'd been together once but were now detached.

Because the left hand refused to accompany the right, the right hand missed its partner. I could tell by the way it played, moving its fingers faster and more expressively, that it was using one flirtatious technique after another to try to be reunited with it. At first the right hand played delicately, pressing its fingertips timidly on the keys as if it were something fragile or naive, something that needed taking care of. Then, because the left hand wasn't moved, its rhythm and volume remaining consistent, the right switched tactics – instead of courting the left's sympathy (or protection, maybe), it feigned indifference, as if attempting to arouse the left's interest through its own lack of it. And when the left hand resisted, the right expressed its unhappiness by playing more gently and delaying the resolution of its leaps of melody to make them sing with special sweetness. In the absence of feeling from the left, the right hand strained its cadences until they seemed so . . . so . . . *How can I explain it?* Well, they seemed so full of feeling. The more the right hand failed to get a response, the more desperate it became. Alone, it played faster, with an almost hysterical speed. Until the climax, when the storm is at its most vicious, where it suddenly became heavy, giving the impression – because it had slowed so much that it was out of sync with the rhythm – of disorientation, as if it were dazed or unable to manage without assistance. The right hand's fingers climbed the keyboard, drifting away from the left, expanding the melodic theme, slowly, by a note or two – tentatively at first, then with resolve – until the strain of the gap became apparent and, worried it had gone too far, the right hand returned to the original melody and tempo (though the high notes lingered in the air, since the sea air had corroded the hammers and deprived the piano of the warmth for which Bechsteins are known). For some time it went on like this, the right hand extending the melody a little further, for a little longer, prolonging the distance between itself and its old companion until, reaching the cadenza, when Chopin fears Sand dead, it held its high note for such a long time that my heart –

worrying that, like a kite that nobody is holding, the melody would not come back down – sped up and I felt certain my left hand would finally *do something*, that it would swell up from beneath the melody and 'catch it'. But it didn't. Obedient to the score, it remained restrained, firm, steady, even-tempered, so resistant to being carried away that it might have seemed cruel had it not at the same time felt somehow comforting, as if the absence of sentiment was not a way for the left hand to distance itself from the right, but the opposite, a way to contain it.

WINTER

Chapter 10

It doesn't look like life, it looks like sea life

I sometimes sat and looked backwards: instead of facing the solarium window and looking at the panoramic part of the view, I'd sit with my back to it and look at the building site. Despite the weather, at eight o'clock each morning the construction site came to life. The workers arrived and started doing things, restoring the large sheets of plastic tacked to the window openings, refilling the ditches in which the matrix of pipes – the skeleton of the sewage system – had been laid. Their activities said *Everything can be made good again*. The bricklaying said *One thing, stacked on another, will amount to something*. In the context of a peninsula that seemed to be slipping into the sea, there was something satisfyingly contrary about the way that, a row at a time, the circular walls were rising from the perfectly square podium. *It's better than the alternative*, said Hannah Kallenbach. *What's the alternative?* I said. *Erosion.*

And it's true; if there's one thing that bored me it was watching the coastline in its losing battle with the sea. I was tired of how the ocean pulled up and subtracted a few inches of shore. I was sick of the gigantic waves pressing so constantly against the harbour wall that I feared one day I'd wake to find it gone completely. I was tired of the mountain dirt tumbling down the mountain, and the stagnating seaweed making the air reek of rotting chicken, and the salt corroding the window frames, how every day the ocean drew things into itself – a sandbag, seaweed, it even swept away two boys (who were later recovered by lifeguards).

Sometimes, with the sun shining brightly through the blueness of a winter's afternoon, I'd go driving. Not for any particular reason or in any particular direction, just heading out for an hour or two until (as happens sometimes when one is tired or has been driving for some time) I couldn't say which direction I was facing or which way was home. I'd start out, as was my habit, along the coastal road, winding my way around the peninsula through seaside suburbs whose names and streets I didn't know. At the beginning the sea would be on my right. In the middle of the ocean was an iron structure – not a building, a large machine for retrieving or measuring things. On my left were churches and B&Bs and retirement homes, their windows hidden behind lace curtains.

Mostly I headed out in the general direction of the city – which is where the coastal road ended up – because I liked the company of the city workers heading home, their routes intersecting with mine at traffic lights and roundabouts. And although I'd sometimes veer inland, through the poorer suburbs, I'd always keep the sea nearby (I couldn't see it but there were seagulls circling overhead) so that if I turned right, before long, I would see it again.

But one day, having lost my bearings in a suburb with rows of identically shaped houses, I arrived in an industrial area somewhere west of the city. It was early evening and traffic was at a standstill. A group of begging children threaded their way down the aisle of cars with a cardboard sign – *Your Kindness Is Appreciated God Bless* – and, because I was frightened of them, I opened my wallet and emptied out a wad of cash, mostly pounds.

I didn't recognise Hannah Kallenbach at first because she looked so different from the Hannah Kallenbach I'd been carrying around in my mind. I might not have recognised her at all were it not for her dangly flower earrings, the ones she had worn when first we met. I was so surprised to see her in the car beside me that I didn't notice the traffic moving until a man behind me hooted, shouting, *You've got a car, now learn how to drive it!*

I lost her for a while and then she drew up beside me again. She wore a blue mackintosh and her hair was wet from swimming or getting caught in the rain. She had an amused expression, as though someone had said something funny on the radio, and was less severe-looking than I remembered, perhaps because she was eating something from a polystyrene box. Perhaps she looked less formidable because she seemed more tanned than before, or more muscular. Or because her hair had grown quite bushy. I felt drawn to her. It was more than just the pleasure of recognition I felt, the pleasure of seeing someone again. She was an attractive woman, I thought. Though perhaps, like the red-brick textile factories and low-rise carpet warehouses beside the road that grew more brooding as the evening approached, it was just the way her face was backlit by the setting sun which gave it a romantic sort of mysteriousness.

When the row of cars moved forward, Hannah Kallenbach looked over at me with the narrow eyes I remembered so clearly. I lowered my head and turned the knobs on the stereo. *Remember*, a man on the radio said, *you are the master of your emotions. At night things feel worse because your power over your emotions weakens.* On another station a lawyer was talking about a man who'd stabbed his wife nine times because she'd told him his kids weren't his and she was going to leave him for someone younger and thinner.

I stayed behind Hannah Kallenbach, indicating when she did, taking her turn-offs. I don't know why I was following her, and the imaginary Hannah Kallenbach, displaced by the proximity of the real one, wasn't there to ensure that every move I made was tracked down and accounted for.

Hannah Kallenbach drove slowly, as if allowing me to keep sight of her tail lights as the streets darkened. Following her had produced a pleasant sensation in me, a kind of lightness, a floating sensation, the sort of dizziness you get from singing or the weightlessness which makes someone who is happy or travelling very fast say, *It feels like I'm flying.* I turned right and left along the grid of city streets, which narrowed eventually, until the buildings got shorter and further apart and their vertical thrust gave way to jacaranda branches curving over me, which made the streets feel less like streets and more like tunnels leading to another world. I knew I was driving badly – I nearly knocked over an old man crossing the road with a crutch – but I had the feeling that I was not in charge of where I was going, that I was being moved by something, something bigger than me, as one gets carried along by faith or a body of ideas, so when he swore at me I just shook my head as if to say that it wasn't me driving and I couldn't be expected to take any responsibility for it. Swathes of time passed in which I couldn't say where I'd been or what had happened around me. I tried to concentrate. *Eyes, do your work!* I said, as though my eyes weren't automatically watching where I was going, as though without instruction they might stray off or spend too long looking at the signs beside the road.

Hannah Kallenbach pulled into her driveway and got out. I ought to have gone home but I parked at the end of the street and followed with my eyes as she made her way to the front door and disappeared behind it. I remained for some time, not starting the car, with one hand still resting against the steering wheel, the other on the gearstick. From time to time I sighed as if deciding to leave but when I tried to reach for the keys my hands ignored me. Several times I thought, *Alright, I'm going to switch on the ignition now*, but I'd just sit there watching the large drops of water dislodged from the leaves of the tree above me joining the existing rivulets on the windscreen. Then I fell asleep, or rather tried to, because although I was sleepy and let the blinds of my eyes draw shut (*Not for too long*, I thought, *I'll just blink for a moment*), the seatbelt was pushing into my back and the flashing red light of the immobiliser stood in resistance to my exhaustion.

Then I was in my parents' house. The memory was from childhood, and so distant and so long forgotten that I thought for a moment it belonged to someone else. My father was away on a business trip and I'd come into the living room to find my mother sitting cross-legged on the Persian carpet in front of the fire. A record was playing – Chopin's *24 Preludes* – a plaintive melody with rippling chromatic harmonies, underscored by a sequence of repeated quavers. The lights were off but the fire had turned the walls a pinky-orange colour. She was smoking, tossing her butts into the grate and watching them disappear, mesmerised, as if finding there something meaningful, the way stargazing makes the galaxy seem comprehensible and small. Over and over, as the pianist reached the final notes, she lifted the needle and returned it to the beginning. *Why do you like that piece so much?* I said, and she, noticing me, started, and replied, *Because when I'm listening to it I feel as though I'm in the company of somebody with such a great capacity for understanding – I feel so understood – that I don't want to be without him.*

A woman walking her dog was staring at me as though there was something about me which was deeply interesting or didn't make sense. Afraid that she would ask what I was doing there – to which I had given no thought – I opened the door without knowing where I would go. I wandered along the avenue, peering into the windows of the houses, imagining that if I lived there my life would be somehow better than it was. I imagined which house would be mine: not the one with hanging baskets suspended from every window and railing, not the one with the unkempt front lawn, not the one with the beaded curtain hanging over the upstairs window. From behind the leafy hedges and wide expanses of cut lawn, the houses' lit windows looked warmly at me. Most of the windows were closed but not all of them. In one house a woman stood at the window smoking a cigarette while having a conversation on the phone, the only part of which I caught was, *Let's be honest, you take a hundred different pills every night.* In another, a man was complaining to his wife about his job. *I mean,* he said, *I'm interested in education, I'm interested in upliftment, I'm interested in transformation . . . But sometimes I want to just say fuck it! Fuck everyone and everything involved. Sometimes, I want to just move to America and* be somewhere. *Oh, Fred,* came the reply, *sometimes you say the most outrageous things. Where else could we have a borehole in our garden? Not in Chicago, I'll tell you that much.*

There was a light drizzle, not enough to stop me from being outside. I stood for a while at Hannah Kallenbach's house. Did she live alone? I didn't entertain that hope since to do so would have required entertaining its opposite. What, anyway, did I want from her? *I don't want anything*, I told myself, but what I wished for was a reason, some pretext, to ring the doorbell. The house's exterior provided very little information about what was going on inside it, though from time to time, when a light came on in one of the windows, I could see which room she was in; and sometimes, because of the size of the window or some other clue (I knew, for example, that the upstairs window belonged to a bathroom because steam rose from a pipe poking out beneath it), I could guess at what she might be doing. Once I did get a flash of Hannah Kallenbach herself. She appeared briefly in a lighted window to pick up something that looked like a printer-ink cartridge from the windowsill and I thought, *Remember the little bird!* because she cupped her hand over the cartridge with an unexpected tenderness. For a moment, before she pulled the curtains closed, she presented her face to the window and, producing a box of throat lozenges from the pocket of her jacket, sucked one, tilting her head to one side. The way she looked out at the street through the narrowing aperture of her eyelids, as if to sharpen her gaze and pierce the night more deeply, reminded me of the way people looked at me after concerts, their quizzically knowing expressions – too personal, too urgent, too high up the emotional register – giving the impression that they'd seen right into me. Hannah Kallenbach's look had a strange effect on me. I felt a wave of inexplicable excitement. It was a Wagnerian feeling – luxurious, exorbitant, overstated – yet at the same time it was a physical feeling, rather than a real feeling, as if I'd been excited in the *scientific* sense of the word, as though all the atoms in my body had been heated up and were jumping around. I felt excited but I didn't *feel* excited. It was just, I thought, one of the brain's inexplicable reflexes. And although the source of excitement was far from sexual, it was there, rather than in my brain or my arm or any other organ, that it suddenly expressed itself, so that my hand rushed to my trousers and pressed down, not to fan the feeling so much as to confirm it, the way you press on a sore tooth to bring out the pain.

If the presence of Hannah Kallenbach had excited me, then a few minutes later, when she closed the curtains, the feeling was replaced by a disappointment, the descent into which was so steep and sudden that it produced a sort of vertigo. I stopped on the pavement, looking down. *What's this?* I said. Because there was something on the road. A small creature, hidden almost. *A frog!* I said, as though it were strange to see a frog, as though it were strange such things as frogs even existed in the world. With slow steps, so as not to frighten it, I approached the frog. But it didn't move, even when I was standing right next to it. I bent over and touched it with a twig. *Get out of here*, I said. *Go, before you get run over*. But the frog just lay there, camouflaged by the dim light on the concrete. I poked it a few times with the stick on its back and on its head but still the frog didn't flinch. From behind a group of dustbins chained up outside one of the houses came a rustling sound: a dog was lifting its leg on the bins. It was a small dog, black, some kind of terrier, perhaps. *That's disgusting*, I said to the dog who looked up at me with a begging expression, wanting something, company perhaps, because when he was done he came over to me and looked down at the frog with his head cocked. *Is it a stone?* the dog seemed to be saying. *It's grey and round like a pebble. So is it a stone?* I leant in and prodded the frog again with the twig. This time the frog dragged itself towards me on its front legs as though there were something wrong with its back legs or its hips. I saw a dink in its back. *Oh no*, I said, *its spine is broken. We should put him out of his misery.* But I didn't have the right implement for it, so in the end I just took an empty pizza box from the chained-up dustbins and slid it under the frog, thinking at least to take it somewhere more peaceful to die, but the moment I lifted the pizza box the frog mobilised itself and leapt off into the night.

That night I slept deeply and had the most exquisite dreams. In the first, I was sitting alone on a balcony somewhere drinking a glass of light red wine whose name, according to the label, was *Mazurka, Polonaises.* Then somebody sat down on the chair opposite me. Who was it? In the dark I didn't immediately recognise the face of Belinda Carrots. *Excuse me*, I said, *I'm expecting somebody.* But instead of leaving she started crying. *What have you done?* she said. *What have you done with my Mazurka?* Then she reached over and

I felt certain she was reaching down with her hand to seduce me but the table had become a piano and she was reaching under the keyboard in order – so she said – to feel the underside of the keys. *Sometimes when you're coming at something difficult*, she said, *it's easier to come at it from underneath. When you play the underside of the piano*, she said, *you activate its capacity for feeling.* Then she played something very beautiful. In the next dream, which appeared to be an extension of the first, I was asleep in bed – thus far the dream accorded with reality – when I felt someone prodding me. I opened my eyes and found that several people were in my bed, having some kind of dispute. I was lying on my back with my legs open, like a specimen being observed by a team of scientists. *Is he a man?* a woman was saying. I recognised Hannah Kallenbach as the person speaking. *Hmm*, said someone else. *Hmm . . . let me see.* Hannah Kallenbach said something and everyone laughed. *We know that he has a stomach*, she said, *and lungs, and intestines. But of the many things conceivable about him, we know least about the ones concerning his heart.* I could see that they were poking me between my legs and in my abdomen with some kind of stick but I couldn't feel anything. *We know that once he felt differently*, she said, *but not lately. These days, he mostly feels the same.*

Chapter 11

This dog is love and he was made for love

The infatuation with Hannah Kallenbach did not immediately blossom into the obsession it would become. It began with being asleep or trying to find ways to be asleep. When I woke up I didn't feel as though I was awake. How can I explain it? It was like jet lag or coming round from an anaesthetic. I'd sleep through my alarm and still be so tired that, having struggled to open my eyes, I myself and everything around me was just pale and lifeless shadows. *What's the matter with me*, I'd say to myself. *You're hibernating*, Hannah Kallenbach would reply. *But am I an animal?*

The first thing I'd wake up feeling wasn't sadness. The second feeling was sadness and wishing to be tired again because I was so tired of being sad. Sometimes I felt so sad that I imagined lying down on the train tracks and going to sleep, if only I'd the energy for it. All morning I'd swing between exhaustion and excruciating sadness, which made my eyes close, one more so than the other. I stared at things. I stood for hours at the window until the brilliance of the sun reflecting off the sea's surface made it necessary to turn away. I stared out at the tower until its height, or maybe its empty core overlooked by twenty or so half-finished floors – *What could a person do in such a space?* – issued a morbid invitation, or at least, invited morbid imaginings. I avoided the chaise because I seemed not to sit down so much as collapse into it, and when it slid back it was so comforting just to lie there that I thought I might never get up again. The important thing, I decided, was to stay vertical. My philosophy was to never get comfortable; to sit only on chairs, for example, that would make me want to stand up again.

It was an intimate tiredness, always close by. Wherever I went, at whatever time of day, it accompanied me. The tiredness overwhelmed all desire except itself – the desire to sleep – and the desire to eat, neither of which were *real desires*, since I never expended enough energy to require either. I woke up in order to eat and when I'd eaten there was nothing left for me to do except lie down again. I would straighten my shoulders and widen my eyes, pulling the skin back from the eyeballs, and try to read, but my eyes just slid down over the words, slumping to the bottom of the page as if they hadn't the strength to hold themselves up.

In the afternoons following my visit to Hannah Kallenbach, I didn't immediately, just before dusk – at what photographers call *the magic hour* when everything goes luminous – go down to the car and start driving. I might have kept up the driving, had it not been for the tiredness. One afternoon, having avoided it for days, weeks, months, even, I opened the piano lid, which took such effort that all my hand had the energy for was a few arpeggios before my wrist collapsed and my fingers began trudging up and down the keys as if sunk to the knuckles in mud. Outside, children were playing on the street. I was slumped over the keyboard. *What kind of man goes to sleep with the sun still up*, I thought, but I just felt so tired. *I think it's reasonable to be tired sometimes*, said Hannah Kallenbach, and my shoulders curled. *Descend lower*, she said, and I rested my head against the piano, with one cheek against my left hand, which had not moved from the keyboard. *You're nearly there*, she said – wherever that was – and I closed my eyes as if to better hear the piano's inner workings, the wood on metal, the felt on strings. *Just for a moment,* I told myself. *I'll just close my eyes for a moment, then I'll be fine.* But as soon as I closed my eyes I didn't feel remotely tired. I felt that odd sexual feeling, that reflex that had something in common with the urge to cry or, since it was in my lower body, the need to pee – like the urge to pee, only more precious somehow. It was a strangely feminine feeling, to feel sexual so deep inside the body, so I tried to ignore it, which of course made it more insistent, and it soon occurred to me that perhaps it wasn't the feeling preventing me from going to sleep but the opposite, that the sleepiness had come to stifle it.

Thereafter the tiredness disappeared, so I resumed the sad and stupid business of driving around, which I'd given up for some time. *Where are you going, Mr Field?* Hannah Kallenbach would ask. And I'd say, *Huh?* or, *What?* or, *Who cares?* or, letting my sentences trail off, *Wait and see, wait and see . . .* I didn't have an answer to Hannah Kallenbach's question but I must have been going somewhere important because I'd make an effort with my appearance – an ironed shirt and a clean pair of jeans – then get into the car and drive as if on autopilot, not knowing where I was going yet nonetheless resisting my destination by lingering at traffic lights and turning left at one intersection then right at the next, left and right, right and left, until, having driven around in circles for some time, I'd so thoroughly lost my bearings that when I entered the secretive tree-lined tunnels of Hannah Kallenbach's suburb, I was genuinely surprised.

Every night I'd park in the same spot and observe the houses around Hannah Kallenbach's house, whose proximity to one another, like a sequence of numbers or a set of sisters, suggested an association to each other, as though I might, from one house's story, be able to infer something about the story of the others. At the end of each day, as the sky let go of the last bits of mauve, I'd leave the car and make my way along the street, studying the activities of Hannah Kallenbach's neighbours. I'd examine how, nightly, from between the large, gold, eagle-topped gates of the house beside hers, a red-lipsticked woman would appear muttering, *This way... This way... This way* to the long-haired dachshund scuttling – so it appeared to me – like a windswept old wig along the pavement behind her. And passing the next house, a Georgian-style building with a glass addition after Mies van der Rohe appended to one side of it, I'd stop to listen for the man within practising opera somewhere out of sight. And coming to the end of the row, I'd pay attention to the comings and goings of the nun from the old house in whose window, most nights, a large cat positioned itself on a windowsill beside a poster of a lost cat that looked very much like itself.

So it was, that although in one way I didn't know them at all, in another way, over time, I came to feel that I knew the inhabitants in a peculiarly intimate way. Occasionally I saw the private scenes one hopes to see when one is snooping around in the dark: a woman holding up a pair of panties in her hand, a man with no clothes on switching on the kettle. But mostly the vignettes unfolding inside the houses exposed only the dull activities of domestic life: people cleaning up, people loading washing machines and rearranging things, opening drawers, motioning for each other to see things on computer screens. Even the fragments of conversation which filtered out from the houses were less the intense and meaningful private exchanges I'd imagined people who knew each other well would have when they were alone than repetitions of well-worn phrases like *Uh huh* or *Let's not argue about that* overlaid – as in the rattle of film projectors accompanying old movies – by the tranquil, even-tempered beeps of fax machines and dishwashers finishing up their cycles.

One night, having made my inspection of the row of houses, I went further than I'd gone before and came to the end of the avenue where there was a graveyard, the old kind in which different members of a family are buried together. Dandelions grew between the graves. I walked around looking at the inscriptions on the headstones. It seemed to me that people who loved each other died close together. There was, for instance, a headstone for a wife who had died at forty-six and her husband only a year after. Below the husband's name were the names of the couple's children, two of them, who had died forty years later. And then, having run out of space on the main stone, there was a second stone, smaller, on which, on its own, appeared the name of a third daughter. This headstone was not standing upright in the ground but was laid flat over the grave and covered in cling film as if to stop it from being damaged by the weather.

The graveyard was so devoid of life that when I encountered the little black dog I took him at first for a hole in the ground. Despite his sodden pelt, which clung to him, making him look very thin, the dog had a haughty air, as if he wasn't a stray dog or a feral dog but a lost dog, a beloved pet who'd come apart from his owner. I called the dog to follow me and although I could tell from his demeanour that he'd heard me, because he lifted his ears to receive the call and cocked his head slightly, he just sat there beside the grave as if in obedience to an order to stay.

After that I often encountered the dog on my journeys. If he wasn't in the graveyard he would be on the verge, lying upturned with his legs splayed in the air, or sitting with a slobbery tennis ball in his mouth which he'd occasionally drop, letting it roll away from him for a while before chasing it. Sometimes, among the sound of my footsteps, I'd hear small rustling sounds, the sounds of a second journey accompanying mine, and a second later the black shape of the dog would appear, darting after a rabbit or a cat. I could tell from his expression that the dog recognised me but whenever I called to him he just lifted his nose as if to catch a scent and looked at me with his little black eyes from behind his overgrown fringe.

Once, having not seen the dog in his usual places, I went looking for him down a path that led from the far end of the graveyard to an alley running behind the row of houses. I hadn't gone far when I found the dog sitting in front of a fence. He sat in an oddly human pose, coquettish almost, like a small child, with his back legs stretched out in front of him in a Y-shape. It was raining and the dog was staring at the fence growing gradually darker with wet, his body so full of tension that his leg and even his lower jaw trembled. *What are you looking at?* I said, because the fence was so covered over with ivy that I didn't immediately see the place, towards the middle, where a section of wood, from age or accumulated rotting, had come away from the wood around it. I tested the wood. It flexed easily and the dog seemed pleased because his tail swept against the ground.

There was a rock in front of the fence, and by putting one foot on the rock I could climb through. So it was that I, who had never thought of doing such a thing, crept into Hannah Kallenbach's garden like a no-good animal. The perimeter of the property was lined with tall plants – bushes and reeds and medium-height trees – at the far end of which, behind a flowerbed populated by leafy ferns and agapanthus, a light was on, making visible the house looming over the garden. There were two ways to get to it: directly, along the wavy gravel path which crossed the large central lawn; or the long way, circling towards it through the plants, which had the advantage of being both hidden and sheltered (the light drizzle hadn't penetrated the densely packed foliage) but required one to go down on one's hands and knees along the ground, which was covered with rancid, wet leaves. I manoeuvred through the darkness like a monkey, feeling that I could see the house without being seen by it. In this way I came right up to the windowsill and stationed myself beneath an unappealing window plant – a succulent with pointy flowers and fleshy leaves.

How can I convey the fondness I felt for that room? Explaining it wasn't the point. What mattered was just to be near it somehow. So I sat there, dead still, until some time later when, after an hour or so, the curtain shifted and then settled again, leaving a sliver of yellow light exposed. I couldn't see the peripheries of the room (because the gap between the curtains, as in a peep show, revealed a little, hiding the rest from view) but from what I could see, everything in the room was exactly the same as it had been: the string-bound chair still facing the window, the heavy wooden desk piled with the same arrangement of papers. Even the two spiders I'd seen on my first visit were still dangling from their long legs in the corner of the room. The lamp on Hannah Kallenbach's desk was angled upwards, towards the painting after Chagall, in which I now saw, hidden among the three figures – the woman, dog and house – a small figure, a very small figure, standing in the doorway of the house. *Was it a man?* It looked like a man, although I couldn't be sure because the picture was some distance from me and because his trousers, in the painting's characteristically sketchy way, had been drawn without a line in the middle so they looked like a skirt. Whereas the other characters in the picture were looking sideways, to the left and right over the rim of the picture as if at something out of sight (at the larger scene from which the one on the canvas had been extracted), the man, resting one hand against the doorframe, was staring directly ahead, looking out of the picture at me.

When Hannah Kallenbach came in, everything went luminous – first the room, and then everything. She was *electric*, I thought, the kind of person whose presence is *electric*, like a man or woman who is either so beautiful or so charismatic that they *light up a room*. She crossed the room and sat down, fastening her scarf more tightly around her. It was a red scarf with a tiny silver thread running through it. For a moment nothing happened, then her head turned. What was she looking at? The man who'd just come in. When he sat down, the sliver of room between the curtains hid his face from view but I could see his shoes. They were black shoes, lace-up, sombre, elegant, the kind of shoes an art dealer might wear, or a socialite, or someone who eats at expensive restaurants, but also somehow childlike, since they gaped slightly at the sides like the shoes of a schoolboy too impatient to untie the laces.

The air outside the window was full of creatures, the kind you only hear when it rains, so I pressed my face right up to the glass to hear better. They were making small talk, he asking if she had been well, she returning the question. *For me*, he complained, *there is no doubt that every day things are getting worse. Every day I wake up feeling worse than the day before. Every day I feel certain that today's the day it's going to happen. That what will happen?* Hannah Kallenbach said. *I don't know . . .* the man said dully. *That I'll vomit or start screaming or run around cutting the hedges naked.*

Since the man couldn't be apprehended directly, the only thing I had to go on, apart from his shoes, was his voice. *What the hell, what the hell*, he said. *Do you know what? Last night I found myself at the telephone with the receiver in my hand and no idea who I was trying to call.* He had a flat, affectless voice and relayed his complaints in a detached, operational tone, like a professional. *The night before*, he said, *I woke up standing over the dustbin about to urinate.* Again he spoke haltingly, as if reading his words off a sheet of paper. *I'm lost*, he said. *Not geographically, of course, I mean I know where I am, but I'm never where I'm meant to be. Sometimes I think the only way I'll ever get what I want is if I come across it by accident.*

After that his voice lowered and became inaudible, but I'd stopped listening anyway because the dog, who must have dug his way under the fence, appeared. Only this time he came right up to where I was sitting and, as is typical of dogs, dug his nose into the seat of my trousers which, since a person is not without sensation in that region, produced a response that was inappropriately sexual. *I just want to sit down and think*, the man was saying from behind the curtain. *Think about what?* said Hannah Kallenbach. And he said, *Everything. Just everything.* Catching hold of the dog by the scruff of his neck, I pushed him away, legs outstretched, belly to the ground, into the bushes. His hair looked wiry but was in fact surprisingly soft to touch. The dog wriggled out of my grasp and darted a few feet back, not because he was afraid but because he thought we were playing a game and was, in this way, enticing me to chase him. We must have made a noise because the window opened. *Ssh*, said Hannah Kallenbach. *There's someone outside.* Her hand appeared at the windowsill. *Hello?* she said. The man's hand appeared beside hers, elderly, spotted, protruding from the sleeve of his jacket. *Hello?* he said. And then, *There's nothing there, or if there is you won't see it . . . Fucking foliage.*

I stayed beneath the windowsill until the light went

off and everything was quiet. The dog, having given up on his game, lay down some distance away and went to sleep. As I left, I don't know why, I lifted the dog awkwardly – it was like wrenching something up from the ground – and carried him to the fence. At first he struggled but then, tired of resisting, he let himself be carried, albeit stiffly, through the hole in the fence, down the alley to the car, where I opened the door and put him on the passenger seat, manoeuvring his legs into a position which made him look less unwilling to be there. The dog was compliant now, allowing himself to be rearranged, and I allowed myself to believe that he was as comfortable as he now looked. Perhaps he *was* more at ease, because he let me dry off his fur and each foot with my coat, even his underbody, rubbing the lining over his chest and up along his forearms. *What have I done?* I said, and the dog looked up at me from the passenger seat as if to say, *You're asking me?*

At home, I undressed in the bathroom because, for some reason, I wanted to avoid being seen naked by the dog. I was curious about the man's relationship to Hannah Kallenbach. There was an intimacy between them, yes, but not a category of intimacy I recognised. I had the idea that they might be colleagues, or have some kind of professional association. What kind of profession I couldn't say, but I lingered on this possibility anyway to displace other possibilities, like the possibility that they were married. *Because you want to be married to me*, said Hannah Kallenbach. She seemed to know where I'd been because she said, *Was I as you expected? No*, I said. *Were you disappointed?* she said. *Yes*, I said. *What do you want from me?* she said. *To stay with me? To come away with me on holiday? To live with me in my house?*

Then a bolt of lightning struck the metal roof of a house somewhere out of sight, turning the sky bright blue. The storm must have been nearing because it was only a second before the clap of thunder followed. There was another bolt of lightning and a thunderclap, only this time the thunder came more quickly and it didn't sound like a clap, it sounded like something breaking, like a stone splitting in two, and it was so loud that it sounded twice, first in itself, then in the house's roof and windows which hummed, reverberating from the vibrations of the pressure it released. Is it true that thunder sucks oxygen from the air? That would explain my sudden light-headedness. The dog looked afraid so I patted the edge of the duvet, inviting him to join me, and he rocked back and forth, preparing to launch himself, and after failing several times to jump high enough to land on the bed, lay down beside it on the floor. *There's no moon*, I said, because the clouds were heavy and had covered it over. Then the rain restarted, only this time it was really pelting down, as if the clouds had learnt to let go and now they couldn't stop. But there was something comforting about the sound of the rain from inside the house, especially since I was in bed and not planning on going anywhere. And in the aftermath of the cruel white light, everything looked warmer – the night sky was luminous, almost yellow, and the walls of the bedroom had turned not yellower, but an uncomfortably bodily colour, something between a rich off-white and a jaundiced cream, like the hue of sallow skin or pus or semen.

Chapter 12

Animal pragmatism

After the power lines came down, life was very slow. Trains stopped and traffic lights became four-way stops. The bay was subjected to a schedule of blackouts during which locals, gathered around candlelit tables, said that electricity was bad and they were better off without it. Progress on the site was non-existent. *What's this? What's this? What's this?* Touw would shout as he circled the tower on his daily inspections, his voice echoing through the empty floors. *Get this out*, he'd shout. *Get this the hell out of here!* Then would come a crash as a dead pigeon or faulty bathroom fitting landed in the middle of the building, a giant dustbin whose contents, I thought, must by now rise so high that you couldn't see the ground.

The weather reached an equilibrium: clouds settled over the mountaintop and the sea's surface was taut. In the morning the water seemed impenetrable but by late afternoon two kinds of seaweed started to appear. Days opened up with nothing inside them. The hours seemed huge and far apart. Aside from the window, the dog was my only contact with the outside world. Since I didn't know his name, I called him Schubert because of his tormented character and because, like Schubert, he had dark curly hair. I tried to train him but his overwhelming attitude was defiance. He'd watch me with that cocked head of his, ascertaining what I wanted from him only in order not to do it. He wouldn't come when called, wouldn't fetch a ball and was impossible to take anywhere because he picked fights with other dogs and nipped the heels of passers by. I managed to teach him two basic commands: *sit* and *lie down*, though the two instructions seemed linked in his mind so it was not possible for him to lie down from standing nor to sit for more than a few seconds without lying down.

In the evenings, with no electricity and nobody to talk to, I'd leave the house and go driving. I'd assumed that my evening driving routine would taper off. It was hard to watch myself do it. I'd thought that as time passed I'd get tired of going to see Hannah Kallenbach, that putting myself down outside her window, night after night, would become boring. It seemed likely that, as in a story whose sequence of events is always forward-moving, my visits would either progress to some climax or conclusion, or that I, losing interest, would give up and move on. And yet the story of my time with Hannah Kallenbach – because it was a story, and it was a story about time – was impervious to the passing of time. Nothing happened. Perhaps it was the sameness of my visits which made them so compelling. Because unlike in a story where one can never really be *lost* (since it is always apparent that one is either at the beginning, the middle, etc. from the plot arc or the number of pages remaining), my visits to Hannah Kallenbach were always exactly the same, so that I could return each night to the window and *lose myself* in its familiar scene precisely because it was never possible to say where I was in relation to the end.

The more I visited Hannah Kallenbach the harder it got to bring my visiting her to an end, because every time I went to see her – taking the same roads, past the same traffic jams – the further I seemed to embed myself into a routine which had become so habitual and so familiar that it began to seem like the stuff of which my life was constituted. Hannah Kallenbach had disturbed my sense of time: whereas previously time had been structured around going to sleep and waking up (like stories which begin *One morning*, to give the impression that nothing has gone before), now its arc was strung between my comings and goings to Hannah Kallenbach's house. Units of time reoriented themselves accordingly. What had previously constituted life now felt like the gaps between life because life was seeing Hannah Kallenbach and everything else was just waiting. Within ten minutes of waking up, in among the thousand useless thoughts a person wakes up with, I had thought of Hannah Kallenbach. By the time I'd brushed my teeth, the thought of her had occurred to me another two or three times so that sometimes I didn't brush my teeth to avoid thinking of her. The minutes it took to transfer my clothes from the washing basket to the washing machine or to eat breakfast were subtracted from the time remaining until I would see Hannah Kallenbach. The two minutes that passed watching the dog eat his breakfast brought me two minutes closer to seeing Hannah Kallenbach again. All day, whatever I was doing, I was marking time. While I walked between rooms or tried to read or stood around listening to things (like dogs, barking, somewhere on the other side of the street) or lay on the chaise wondering, *What will become of me?* or leant my head on my hand while waiting for the kettle to boil or adjusted the blanket I wore like a shawl around my shoulders or looked outside at the seagulls clinging to the harbour, or the boats, or the movement of the tops of the trees, or counted the kitchen tiles or stared at my watch until it looked like many black hands were overlaying each other or did nothing but watch a speck of fluff drift by for what seemed like an eternity thinking, *So much time has passed*, I was always, at the same time, making complex mathematical calculations about time passing and time remaining and where I was in relation to seeing Hannah Kallenbach again. Because where I was was only where I was in relation to her. Nothing else mattered. The only thing that mattered was when would I get to Hannah Kallenbach's house and when I got there would she be there. The effect of which was that my actual time spent with Hannah Kallenbach (separated by the window) felt meagre, coming felt like going, and my visits soon went from being a source of pleasure to a source of suffering, since no sooner had I sat down outside the window than I'd be worrying about the moment when I'd have to stand up and go back home.

The waiting took up all my energy. I waited by withdrawing energy from everything else. A heavy weight descended on me while I was waiting – the weight of waiting – so that by the time I started driving I was so exhausted that I had to keep myself awake by making a list of things I remembered about the yellow room – the string-bound chairs, mine and hers, the childlike painting by someone after Chagall, the bookshelf with its grand European novels, the mismatched ceramic pots . . . But my tired mind couldn't populate the list and remember it at the same time so the items, not wanting to be catalogued, dissolved the moment they were thought about. I'd park and, with heavy legs, make my way down the alley, turning left and right at the fence to check that the neighbours weren't watching, before climbing cautiously in and making my way as usual through the foliage to my post outside the window.

Sometimes I'd sit for an hour or so, waiting for her beneath the darkened window, and then go home. Other times, as if she'd been waiting for me to come, I'd sit down and almost immediately the light would come on and the curtains would shift, letting me survey the yellow room in which everything – the chairs, the desk, the piled-up papers and ceramic pots – was exactly as I'd left it. Sometimes when the yellow light filled the room

I wanted so much to be inside, and was so close to the realisation of that desire, that I felt quite dismal. Other times, when the light came on, I wanted to go home. Not because I didn't like where I was but because, although nobody had seen me, I felt as though Hannah Kallenbach knew where I was, the consequence of which was that the degree of openness of the curtains took on a special significance. When the gap was wider, as if she'd purposefully left it open for me, the room felt welcoming, but when the curtains were pulled so tightly shut that I could hardly see a thing, the slice of light coming through their frayed edges seemed a rebuke and, ashamed of my skulking around, I wanted to leave. Although I never actually left, because when Hannah Kallenbach came into the yellow room, crossing through the gap between the curtains before sitting down in the chair – *her chair* – beside the window, the room would light up in a warm and inviting atmosphere. *She's so beautiful*, I'd think. Because whereas one tends to forget after a while that a person is beautiful, especially if you see them all the time, Hannah Kallenbach's beauty presented itself to me over and over again. Every time I saw her I felt a kind of pang. Yes, *pang* was a good word for it: like young love or immature love or new love, love but with a tragic aspect.

Sometimes, from somewhere out of sight, I'd hear private noises – plates and cutlery, floorboards, a man saying, *Ooh*, as if hearing something salacious – but I paid them no attention. Sometimes I'd smell dinner cooking but that didn't interest me either. Even the comings and goings of Hannah Kallenbach's male visitor, who must have been her husband because he seemed to live there, only interested me insofar as I wished they wouldn't happen. And some nights, when for some reason the man didn't come into the room or arrived later than usual – because I liked being alone with her, and because a person's absence always equates to death – it would occur to me, just for a moment, if I let myself think it, that perhaps he was dead and I wouldn't have to see him again.

On the evenings when Hannah Kallenbach and the man did sit together, talking, their conversations, from outside, were muffled and it was difficult to make out exactly what was being said. Filtered through the walls of the house, their words led in a number of directions. When the man talked about *the fucking crickets, the fucking crickets*, he could have been talking about *fucking tickets*. The middle syllables were more audible than the outer ones so that words like *fog* could have been *dog*, *deluge* sounded like *delude*, and *weight* and *wait*, *mist* and *missed*, *toupee* and *to pay* were completely interchangeable. The man's frequent references to a *writer* could, depending on what my ear liked, equally have referred to a *rider*. The lack of clarity was confusing, but it left room for fantasy. Sometimes my mishearings were so intriguing that instead of turning my face towards the glass to hear better, I'd turn away as if to help the words lose their shape. I liked the way my ears betrayed me. It liberated the disembodied voices to say what I wanted them to say. Before long my failed attempts to understand went from a source of frustration to one of pleasure. The man's slow way of speaking, with not much moderation in volume, made it easy to erase him since his voice, so robbed of feeling, suggested (like someone on tranquillisers or reading from a script) that he was anyway *not really there*. Allowing me, listening to the apparition of a word filtering through the layers of curtain and glass, to *hear things*, things unrelated to him or his situation, things about myself, so that as I sat outside on the cold flagstones, I was, at the same time, sitting on the string-bound chair in the yellow room. When, after a long silence, Hannah Kallenbach said, *You're deep in thought*, it could have been *You're beautiful* that she said, and because of the strange changing of places that had occurred, it felt like she was talking to me.

Sometimes when I was driving back late at night, I'd

stray onto the wrong side of the road as if forgetting for a moment which country I was in and where was home. The feeling that I was in two places at once infected me at the house too. I'd close the front door and find that sounds coming from outside – a car door closing, a dog crying *Awoo-woo* from across the street – seemed to be coming from within. The rhyming geometries in the entrance hall were disorienting. It was as though the composition of shapes around me – the tightly spiralled staircase against the zigzag ramp, the vertical stripes of the radiator beneath the striated reinforced-glass windows, both overlaid by squares of light coming in through the perforations in the overhead slab – intersected one another in a way that was somehow contradictory and, as in a cubist painting, forced me to occupy several points of view at once.

The dog wasn't a very sociable character. He refused to be picked up or stroked, preferring to spend his time alone, either sleeping or playing with his tennis ball. But when I returned from Hannah Kallenbach's house he would always be lying in the entrance hall waiting for me. Worn down by being alone, he wanted to be loved the way a dog is meant to be loved and would greet me with an uncharacteristically solicitous attitude, covering me with licks and offering up his pink underside to be scratched. And I, who liked those moments of closeness, perhaps because of their infrequency, would bend down to stroke him, making ridiculous declarations of love. To which the dog, wriggling his torso and craning his neck round to face me, responded with an appreciation which I just knew – how can I explain it? – was inappropriate. There was something primitive about the way he moved; it was too joyful, too expressive somehow, more than just doggy enthusiasm. *He's just a dog*, said Hannah Kallenbach. *Dogs are frisky.* It's true, I thought, excitement is different for a dog. A dog's excitement is not just associated with other dogs. A dog is seduced by anything if the shape is right. Table legs, chairs, a handbag . . . They are all the same to a dog.

But really what the dog loved most of all was his tennis ball. Whenever I looked for him he would be in one of two places, either upturned in a patch of sun somewhere or standing at the top of the ramp with the tennis ball in his mouth. He carried the ball around constantly. The only thing he loved more than having it between his teeth was dropping it. He didn't want me to throw the ball for him, preferring to position himself at the top of the ramp where, having opened his mouth, his eyes would accompany the ball's downward journey until the strain of separation became too great and he would set off after it with a scattering of legs. The dog's appetite for this game was untiring; he seemed to want it to go on forever. Long after his muscles ought to have grown tired I'd hear him running back and forth along the ramp, casting the ball away and then retrieving it. Part of me thought, *How can he play this game so constantly without getting bored or tired?* yet on another level his playing made me feel a sort of kinship with him because it expressed something of our own situation, the dog's and mine, since from the moment I got him I'd been afraid of losing him. The idea of it was so bound up with the dog's presence that each time I saw him I couldn't help rehearsing his absence, as though by imagining him not there I might partially master the loss in advance. So that when I watched him going to and fro along the ramp I was also asking myself, *How would it feel to stand here and not see him playing with his tennis ball?* And when I came home and found the dog waiting for me at the door I was also thinking, *What would it be like to come home and not find him waiting for me?*

Sometimes during a power cut the lights would come on in the middle of the night with a surge then go off again. And in the moments before my eyes had adjusted to the dark, when it was hard for things to preserve their shape, I'd see my dressing gown hanging beside the bed and imagine Hannah Kallenbach standing beside me. *Are you OK, Mr Field?* she'd say. And when I opened my mouth it was that small child's voice that replied, *Fuck you*, meaning *Fuck you for haunting me in this way. Fuck me?* she'd say. Sometimes instead of Hannah Kallenbach it would be Touw standing over me, asking, *What have you done? Where the hell is my tower?* with his voice hoarse from shouting. And sometimes in the middle of the night it would be the dog who had climbed into bed with me, and my body, feeling its wet nose sniffing around for a bit of sweaty crotch, would tense up – first the muscles in my calves would tighten, then my knees would begin to stiffen and there would be a sort of trembling in my legs as though tired out from heavy carrying. Even the sluglike movements of my intestines would go rigid and my spongy lungs, like sails filled with wind, seemed straining to burst. And at those times, that 'turned-on' feeling lower down that so outraged me when awake was allowed to progress without resistance to its inevitable conclusion, though at the point where the climax was meant to be – because there was no reason for excitement maybe – the feeling would always turn back on itself, leaving me with a nothing sort of feeling, and I'd wake up moaning, *Nooo*, but it was just the sound of my stomach grumbling.

One morning a little bird was stationed on the branch outside the window, cheeping loudly, as if relieved to be reunited with me after the separation of sleep. The air through the window was thick, almost impenetrable, so it took me a while to notice a second bird standing beside the first one, because it was standing very still on the branch – not preening itself or sunning itself like cold-blooded creatures do, just standing there, quite still, so that it looked almost like part of the tree, like a small grey fruit. Even when, from time to time, the bird twitched or shuddered and buried its head in its feathers, it was almost indistinguishable from the leaves. After a while, thinking me dead or inanimate perhaps, the second bird hopped towards me in a series of jerky movements. Reaching the window, it stopped and looked at me with its dead black eyes. It was making a noise without moving its beak and though I couldn't understand what it was saying I knew that it was communicating, that it was actually *saying something* and not just making senseless noises. *What's the matter with him?* the bird seemed to be saying. *Is he in anguish? No*, said the other bird. *It's agony, actually.*

Has he been tortured in some way?

I think he's a part of the unhappiness that's come apart from the total mass of unhappiness.

Chapter 13

Causa Sine Qua Non

Of course, it happened long ago, but there is an evening I think of all the time. Here it is. The day was nearly over. When I got into the car the sky was so welled-up with colour – orange, yellow, blue, green – that it made me want to vomit. I watched the house disappear in the rear-view mirror, its square body and spindly limbs subsumed almost immediately by the mist. It was hard to look at the road beneath me because the mist drew everything into itself: no more trees, no more houses, one minute the street you're driving on is there, the next you're unsupported.

All day I'd watched it, the fog rolling in. The sight of it was extraordinary, this vast cloud advancing from the ocean. The air was thick and heavy. It drifted in on some current or wind until it came to the edge of the mountain where it stopped and waited, accumulating, hanging over the world like a new law. The trees were pale, so dull you could hardly tell they were there. Houses had their shutters closed against the weather so that it looked as if they were covering their faces with their hands. *What are they ashamed of?* I was thinking. *What are they afraid of?* The trees lining the road were divided into intensities of grey – those nearest were pale, past a certain point everything lost colour. The landscape was dry and arid, as though so destroyed by the cold or the salty air as to no longer be able to bear vegetation. All around were differentiated shades of grey: grey streets, grey houses, fog, trees growing clouds instead of leaves.

Inland, the mist was thinner. I stood for a while at Hannah Kallenbach's fence before climbing in and crawling along the path I'd worn through the bushes. It was dark outside and inside the yellow room it was dark. In the seconds or milliseconds before the light came on, the room was so dark that there was nothing to pin my eye onto. I didn't know the room was occupied until the door opened. *I was worried about you*, said Hannah Kallenbach. *I wasn't expecting you tonight.*

Well, said the man, *here I am.* He was holding his

body differently, speaking differently, his voice strangely caught. Then there was a silence and I wasn't sure if and when he would start talking. But then, having prefaced it with *I'm no good at storytelling, you know*, he sat down and started to tell a long, involved story about a writer, or maybe a rider, it was hard to say because of the way certain sounds came through the window clearly while others were suppressed.

The story was, as it happened, a story I'd heard before, anecdotally, to illustrate the legal problem of assigning culpability in a complicated sequence of events. *As you know*, the man began, *there's a fog outside. It's foggy. Quite foggy. Foggier anyway than it was yesterday and the day before that also. The radio said to stay in*, he went on, *but, fog notwithstanding, I took the tarpaulin off the car. I wanted to go out so it was necessary to drive through the fog. Anyway*, he went on, *the Met Office was saying on the radio that drivers should take care where visibility was reduced to less than ten metres, which was everywhere. Flights and trains had been cancelled, they said. And every minute the veil was getting heavier. It was like being lost in an atmosphere of memories. I couldn't feel the tips of my fingers; my hands were lost in cloud. When I looked down, I couldn't see what shoes I was wearing. On the road, objects disappeared, apart from the aerials of the houses, which for some reason stood out clearly against the sky.*

Every inch and every metre, every block and every street corner, in every conceivable direction as far as the eye could see, had been whited out. I was, as they say, enveloped in this thick layer of cloud. I was in a daze. I kept thinking it was me, that the reason I couldn't see anything was because I wasn't looking hard enough. I had the idea that the vagueness in my head had entered my body. You know how it is to stand up too quickly and see your eyes covered for a moment by a film of blank? She didn't answer. *Well that's how it felt. Only sometimes things disappeared and reappeared, and sometimes they disappeared completely.*

The tree beside me knocked its branches lightly on the windowpane as if asking to go in, its yellow speckled leaves made a sighing sound as they moved, and the man's subdued voice gave way to silence. The silence made me nervous because I didn't know what it was saying. Because it wasn't the kind of silence that is deep and empty, it was the kind that is full and alive. *Well,* said Hannah Kallenbach, *what happened then? I just kept on driving,* the man said. *There wasn't much traffic so I went slowly, trusting that whatever was ahead of me would become clearer the nearer I got to it. It felt dangerous to be driving, but the fog pulled me into itself and I surrendered to it because the air quality was entertaining – telling stories about temperature, meteorological conditions, these kinds of things.*

Then, some way from home, along the highway, I saw something: a shape, a vague outline. Dimly, only very dimly. Then it disappeared. Well, that's how it seemed to me, he said, *although of course a thing that actually exists can't just vanish into thin air. It was a big black animal-type thing,* the man said, *maybe a horse but maybe not. Unlikely to be a horse, I thought, because what kind of horse rides on a highway? But the air was full of uncertainty. All that was certain was that I had no idea if or when or where I would find something.* And then, indicating that he had reached the heart of the story, the man stood up. I could see from his shadow that he was walking to and fro in the single-windowed room. *I turned off somewhere,* he said. *I'm not sure where exactly but it must have been the mountain road. I couldn't see the road itself, and as I drove higher – because of wind speed or direction – the air was getting murkier. And I must have forgotten to change gear because at some point the car stalled and when I restarted it in first, the incline was too steep and it couldn't manage. So I pulled up the handbrake and stopped. The* road was empty. It was as though the mist had eaten up the other cars, like some kind of acid or a devouring white gas. Twice I tried to start the car but it just rolled backwards, so then I turned it off and didn't try again. It looked as though the landscape was breathing and because I couldn't really breathe, I had the feeling it was sucking the breath out of me. I felt tired and pleasant thoughts floated into my mind.

It sounds frightening, Hannah Kallenbach said. And dangerous, to be stopped like that, broken down in the middle of the road. You might have started a pile-up.

But what could I do about it? the man said. Nothing. It was a breakdown. There was nothing to be done about it. I just sat there, waiting. And after a while, when I looked up, something opened in the sky. It was drizzling slightly, a sunlit drizzle. The late-winter flowers beside the road were like bits of snow. The trees which had been Pompeii-like, as if covered in ash, were being released from their shroud, regaining colour. The afternoon sun, softened by the thin layer of cloud, cast everything in a luminous light. It was beautiful, he said, a kind of miracle.

Anyway, he said, as the cloud burned off, ahead of me, not too far away, trotting to one side of the road, I saw the horse again. It was definitely a horse because

*this time I could see the rider's figure rising and lower-
ing above it in jagged counterpoint to the trot. And the
funny thing is,* he said, *the horse seemed to be watching
me. It seemed, all the while, as it was riding, for some
reason to be turning its head around to get a look at me,
staring at me with its big black eyes as if it was trying to
tell me some secret, as if it was using its eyes to commu-
nicate some message, like a prisoner under surveillance,
like maybe that it was being pulled along by the rider
in a direction it didn't want to go in. Only the horse
was turning towards me so urgently and so frequently
that, as happens when you're not watching where you're
going, it began veering off course, stumbling at first into
the roadside ditch, and then, panicked, trying to right
itself, turning back, but too sharply, crossing over the
yellow line on the side of the road, perpendicular to the
direction of traffic, leaning its neck forward and acceler-
ating into a canter.*

*I had a vision of somebody – me, I suppose – crashing
into it. And I was so caught up with worry,* the man was
saying, *that I didn't see that another car actually was
coming until, having swerved to avoid colliding with
me, it overtook me and headed directly for the horse.*

Oh, how awful, said Hannah Kallenbach. *Oh no.*

At the last minute, the man said, *the horse lifted its legs and jumped as if to clear the roof of the car. I crouched over the steering wheel – a sympathetic reflex, I guess – then sat up again. The rider was sitting a few feet in front of me on the road, breathing heavily into the cold air. There was no blood on his face, which I was grateful for, just a bit of brown stubble and an expression that was almost bemused. Perhaps it was gratitude.*

Thank goodness, said Hannah Kallenbach. *It's amazing how many people get hit by cars without dying.*

Cars stopped and an ambulance appeared from nowhere, the man said. *I couldn't see it but I knew it was there because there were blue freckles of dirt appearing and disappearing on the windscreen. Somebody covered the rider with a blanket. He had propped himself up on his elbow. I looked around for the horse, which I found lying across the road on its back. The car which had hit the horse – it was some kind of Volvo – had shorn off all its legs below the knee, so that the horse was swaying from side to side on its back, not understanding why it couldn't get up, not knowing why it was rolling around like a fruit, never able to get enough momentum to turn itself upright. A small crowd had gathered around the horse, which had turned again to look for me, and having found me was staring at me through the gathering of legs. I could see from its expression that the horse was thinking, that it was thinking of someone, because it had the look of a creature who is not alone but has someone to think about. Then it closed its eyes.*

To die? asked Hannah Kallenbach.

No, the man said, *just to think. A police car had arrived and a woman was asking the policeman to put the horse out of its misery but the policeman said he couldn't shoot animals. She asked the paramedic to give the horse a shot of something to kill it but of course the paramedic couldn't give medicine to animals either. Well, was there a vet, then? she wanted to know, which there wasn't.*

Of course not, said Hannah Kallenbach.

The upward inflection of Hannah Kallenbach's *Mmm* meant, *And what happened then?* But the man said, *Nothing happened. The bystanders were dispersing. It was clear to everybody, I suppose, that the drama was over, that there was no more excitement. The rider just sat there drinking a glass of water and the horse just lay there swinging its torso from side to side over the ridge of its spine, trying to get up. Its lips were pulled up over its gums and from time to time it made a sound that, if it were human, I'd have called a sigh. The rider's face was white because when he'd heard what had happened to the horse he'd thrown up.*

What a story, said Hannah Kallenbach.

But the story wasn't over. *There was something odd about him*, the man went on. *He was odd-looking. One thing that was odd about him was that he wore the same shoes as me! I'd noticed it earlier, but it was only now that I noticed his black trousers, which, though they were slightly darker and looser around his legs, were also the same as mine. As, when I took in his whole outfit, was his dark-green jumper with buttons on the sleeves. And his short brown tweed coat with big lapels, into whose pockets he reached his hand and withdrew, nestled together in a neat cream ball, a slightly less dirty and frayed, but unmistakably the same, pair of woollen gloves that I'd brought back from a trip to India. Several times, as he sat there, he buried his gloves in his pocket and retrieved them. Anyhow, a barricade had been set up by then and the police were trying to clear traffic. Keep moving, said the policeman who came up to my window. So I started the car and after a few goes managed to get going. I remember that the rider, as I passed him, was sitting with his neck at an odd angle, visualising the rest of the horse perhaps, because his eyes kept flickering off in the direction of the legs. If he spent too long sitting like that, I thought, his neck would get stiff. But perhaps he had whiplash. Who knows? For a moment our eyes met and although he'd put on a grimace, I had the idea that his mouth wasn't expressing anguish or pain, that he'd pulled his lips that way to hide something, a smile maybe, the way a person might cough to cover up a laugh. I looked at the rider hard as I passed,* the man said, *marking the differences between us. His hair was brown, like mine, but shorter. If his well-kempt appearance was anything to go by, he had money. And although his clothes were different from mine – newer, straighter, better-fitting – what was so painfully different about us, given that we were essentially the same, was that he was much more handsome than me. That's why I kept my head down as I drove past, protecting him, I suppose, since he'd not have been pleased by the resemblance.*

Now, through the gap, I saw Hannah Kallenbach's hand move towards the man and perhaps she touched him somewhere on his body in a way that surprised him because his foot flinched. *What are you doing?* he said. The hand was suspended for a moment in the gap before it was retracted, and in that time I thought how beautiful it was, that her hand showed its affection beautifully.

Are you OK? she said.

I don't know, he said. *Do I look OK?*

As I drove back into False Bay, a fog lay over the water. Above me, the square white house and the tower behind it seemed, well, not *similar* exactly but connected somehow, or belonging together, sprouting beside each other on the mountain as if grown from the same organic source. I manoeuvred my way along the bends of the coastal road in a state of total exhaustion, listlessness on an unprecedented scale, tiredness to an unprecedented depth. What was wrong with me? How could I explain the nature of my problem when I was such a stranger to myself? How could I possibly grasp what was going on inside me when the inside of my body was hidden from me, walled in by my skin? When it was impossible to feel my organs in the way I could my limbs? As I parked at the bottom of Jacob's Ladder and looked up at the tower, which sat on its podium and looked down at me, I felt profoundly *wrong* – though whether it was my inner mysteriousness which felt wrong, or the feeling that something was mysteriously wrong inside me, was hard to say. *Think*, I told myself. *Think.* And then, looking at the tower, I started thinking. I thought things unrelated to the tower, thoughts about myself. Because suddenly, not in words but in shapes, the tower revealed something to me. It was as if, slowly but clearly, its stacked-up floors, punctured by its central cavity, expressed something of my own situation, as if it had turned my eyes inwards or given my skin a measure of transparency, so that by looking at it, all at once, I could picture my own interior in a way I'd not been able to picture it before. And what I saw, with a sudden vertiginous knowledge, was that what occupied me was not, as I'd thought for all these years, some solid alien presence – like a tumour deep inside, pushing my organs to one side – but a hole. Not a lack, though. Because the feeling of something missing in me, that *I was missing something*, didn't cause me shame or regret. It was a rich feeling. There was a pleasure to be taken in the idea of a body, like a woman's body, with a space in it, a space in which things could be put.

A body with a space in it – once I'd started, nothing could stop me – I thought of it over and over, until the effort of climbing Jacob's Ladder had neutralised the thought, or at least reduced it so that its importance seemed a product of my imagination. *When I get to the top of the stairs*, I consoled myself, *everything will be OK because the dog will be waiting for me.* I had left him alone for a very long time and he would be lonely and thirsty. But when I opened the door, the dog was nowhere to be seen. *Where are you?* I said. *I'm here*, said Hannah Kallenbach. *There's no one here*, I said. *Look!* she said. *In the air!* And when I looked across the entrance hall, past the basin, towards the laundry door, which was slightly open, floating above the floor tiles, almost indistinguishable from the white of the wall, was a veil of white airborne particles.

When I opened the laundry door, among the white flecks of paper hovering in the air was the dog. His eyebrows lifted. He stood under Mim's desk with his black ears flopping out from either side of his head like the leaves of a palm tree. His tail was crooked against the underside of the desk and he had one foot pressed down on Mim's notebook to steady it. White scraps were caught in his whiskers and I could tell from the clicking sound he made as he opened and closed his mouth that paper was stuck to its roof. *What have you done?* I said, and the dog stopped trying to dislodge whatever was in his mouth, put his ears down, and darted out the door.

I reached for him but the dog was faster than me, and cunning. Sometimes, when I'm dredging up the memory of that evening, I think that however much I learn, however much I understand, I know least about why something which one person regards as trivial sends another into the depths of fury. I chased the dog down the corridor. Near the basin he allowed me to close in on him but the moment I tried to grab him he broke away again. He ran up the ramp, with me after him, and although he slowed on the landing, bringing himself within reach, before I could get close enough he doubled back past me and was off. I ran out of breath and stopped. Sensing that nobody was coming for him, the dog stopped too and considered me, his tense body ready to spring at the slightest movement. He yapped, enticing me to resume the chase. Once, twice, we circled the house. Several times he stopped, teasing me, before eluding me, darting sideways, twisting his head excitedly round to check that I was still chasing before, ears back, panting, dashing off again.

Then, caught between two urges – the urge to kill the dog and the urge to run away from him so that I didn't kill him – I stopped. The dog wagged his tail so hard his whole body joined in. *Come here*, I said, making the clicking noise you use to call a horse, and although the dog didn't come – of course he didn't – his guard was let down enough for me to grab him by the collar and bring my hand down on top of his head. Because I'd used my left hand, the blow was like a child's hit, with no real strength in it. But the dog recoiled and looked at me with what appeared, if animals could feel shame, like a kind of humility. I said, *Stand still so I can hit you*, and then switched hands and delivered another puny blow, more a flap than a slap. But I couldn't tell how hard it was because it was cold and I couldn't feel my hands. Anyway, whichever hand I used was equally useless, with neither the power nor accuracy necessary to cause damage.

The dog didn't bark or yelp or bite me. He just sat there with bits of paper poking from his teeth and surrendered. He could have bitten me, I suppose, but in the end a dog is simple and wishes to be loved only. A dog *is* love and a dog is *made for* love. According to animal pragmatism, then, my attack must not have been a form of cruelty but a form of seduction, in the light of which his response was not to retaliate or try to stop me but just to sit there, waiting for the attack to end, as though I'd dispensed it not out of fury or hatred but as a way of preparing him to be loved. And so, when my temper had unwound itself or my serotonin levels had been restored, or both, I said, *I'm sorry* and patted the dog (because a dog can't understand *sorry*), who flinched, then yielded and let himself be comforted.

When I walked away from him he followed me, staying a few steps behind as if wanting always to be in close proximity to me. When I lay in the bath, he stood at the foot of the tub. And when I got out he licked the water off my skin as if the taste of it was me, made drinkable. All night, instead of lying in his basket, the dog paced the room, keeping me awake with the sound of his nails clipping against the floor. He'd stop at the bed's edge, staring at me with his cocked head. *What are you staring at?* I'd say. *I care about you*, the dog seemed to be saying with his eyes. *You concern me. But you're an animal*, I said. *You don't have real feelings.* And the dog said, *I do have real feelings.* Then he lay down and went to sleep, though sometimes he woke momentarily and looked at me – as if to check that I was still there – and having confirmed this, would close his eyes again and resume his ragged breathing.

I lay awake that night for a long time, watching clouds drifting past the window and gathering into thick walls of grey that grew so dense that the sky went milky. By midnight the air was so impenetrable that the window itself had disappeared, the whiteness outside having become indistinguishable from the white wall framing it, as if I were in a windowless room within which nobody would see me or hear from me or think of me again. Except the dog sleeping beside me. I tried not to take too much pleasure in his company, knowing that it was bad to adore him in the way that I did. After all, he was just a dog, a fact that limited my feelings for the dog since I could never really be sure what I was thinking of when I was thinking of him. *What is a dog?* This question occupied all my thoughts. What kind of animal was I dealing with anyway? The animalness of the dog raised two difficult issues. Firstly, is a dog a hairy but essentially human being or is there something more fundamentally different about a dog, making him no more similar to a person than, say, an ant? And secondly, what is a worthwhile way of spending time in life? Or, said another way, what kinds of things are worth investing one's time and feelings in? Sometimes, when I looked down and saw the dog lying on the floor with his legs tucked under him like a grasshopper, I felt an immense affection for him followed by a terrible sadness because it occurred to me that it wasn't a real relationship at all because I'd fallen in love with a grass-hopper. But later, since all kinds of loving feelings flour-ish in the dark, I couldn't help lifting him up onto the bed beside me because the form of affection I most liked (it goes without saying, a man cannot have intercourse with a dog) was just to be curled up against him. And in the middle of the night, woken by the movement of the dog, whose habit was to go round and round and round in circles to warm a patch of duvet before lying down on it, I'd have the bizarre notion that Mim was there, watching me. *What would you do without me?* she'd say. And I'd say, *Just go on living, I guess.*